THE

OTHER

PASSENGER

JE ROWNEY

LITTLE FOX
PUBLISHING

Also by JE Rowney

I Can't Sleep
The Woman in the Woods
Other People's Lives
The Book Swap
Gaslight
The House Sitter
The Work Retreat

For further information,
please visit the author's website.

http://jerowney.com/about-je-rowney

Disclaimer:
This is a work of fiction. All characters, places
and businesses within this novel are works of
fiction and are not based on, or representative
of, real world persons, places, or organisations.

ISBN: 9781739689988

For Freya
Everything happens for a reason.

and Alex
Everything will be

PROLOGUE

She's still looking at me, half an hour after I killed her. Just staring, like she can't believe it.

The air feels heavy, like it's thickened with her disbelief.

My phone's light cuts through the dark, casting long shadows that seem to reach for me. Paranoia. Must be. I don't know how you're supposed to feel when you've done what I have, but being this on edge seems normal, under the circumstances. I'm trying to be rational, trying to reason, but all I can think is *what the hell am I meant to do now*?

The forest around us is dead silent—no comforting rustles or whispers, just a heavy quiet that presses down on me.

My heart's racing, but not from fear. It's the adrenaline, still pumping, refusing to settle. The ground beneath my feet is as hard and cold, unforgiving as my actions. Leaves crunch underfoot as I shift, the sound too loud in the silence. Even though we are out here, far from the nearest town, miles from the last person I saw, the paranoia has me thinking someone is listening, watching. Someone knows what I have done.

The thought makes me turn my head, scan the treeline. There's nothing. There's no one. Even if there was, I wouldn't be able to see. The light from my phone only shines so far. It doesn't reach the skeletal trees. All it lets me see is her face, staring, still staring.

I look down at her again. Those eyes, wide open and accusing, seem to pierce through me. It's surreal, how she just stares, unblinking. I have to move, to do something. But I'm frozen, caught in her gaze as if she's asking me, "Why?"

I should crouch beside her, swipe my fingers over her eyelids. That's what happens on television, isn't it? Somehow I can't bring myself to touch her and bring down the final curtains.

Imagine them picking up my fingerprints from the one part of her I had to touch.

Them. Whoever *They* are. Because there will be a *Them*. Bodies are discovered. Crimes are investigated. Murderers are…

The thought of the word makes a heavy ball form in my throat, and I have to look away, shine my light on the ground. I need darkness. I need this silence. I need a plan.

The chill of the night starts to seep in, a cold reminder of what's done. I can't stand here forever. I've already waited too long.

ONE

Now

David had left with no clear idea of where he was heading, but the further he drove along the slick winding road, the less he cared about his destination. He was going away. That was all that mattered. He was looking forward, focussing on the way ahead, blinkered by the tree line on either side, the edge of the forest beyond. What was behind him was…

There was no need to think about that. The evening faded in his rear view with every mile he travelled. It was meant to have been a celebration, and it had ended up as…

He shook his head, as though trying to dislodge the memory. It had been a disaster from start to finish, and there was still time for things to get worse.

The award was supposed to be his. Malcolm had all but assured him of it. All but. And that was part of the problem. He'd been strung along; made to look like an idiot. Not being recognised was one thing, but being sidestepped and taken for a fool in front of everyone, that was something else. It was intolerable.

David lifted his hands from the steering wheel and slammed them back down with a force that juddered through his exhausted body. He should never have agreed to go; he should never have gone without Amanda.

Shit, shit, shit.

The words formed in his head, but there was no one to hear them, even if he was to let them out of his mouth. There were times, on his commutes to the office, to the sales pitches across the county, to wherever Lottie wanted to be picked up from at whatever time she called on him... There were times that he let his words spill out into the silence, when there was no passenger to hear. Tonight, the only sounds were the hum of the engine, the smooth burr of tyres on tarmac, and the ongoing battle between the windscreen wipers and torrential rain that showed no sign of letting up.

He had driven straight out of Maplewood, leaving the town behind him. Through the suburbs and onwards, up into the moorland forest hills. Five miles, perhaps ten now. No destination, just onwards.

David drove alone so frequently, spent so much time with his hands on the leather-covered steering wheel, that his fingerprints were indelibly etched onto it. Tonight, his usual soft, reverent grip was a white-knuckled clench; the tension channelling through his body singularly focussed on the only outlet it could find, as though the wheel was a lightning rod for his inner turmoil.

His mind a fog, David barely noticed as the needle on the speedometer shuddered past the limit. Even driving uphill, the speed crept up on the deceptive stretches between the bends. There were no cameras out here to clock him, but the sheet rain and moonless night meant that driving conditions were far from optimal. His car was well-maintained, serviced every twenty thousand, all paid for by the company scheme. Even thinking about his workplace made David run his tongue over his lips, trying to rid himself of the sour taste.

A company car, four weeks' vacation and a bonus at Christmas that came nowhere near to covering Amanda and Charlotte's endless wish lists. That was all he was worth. The standard benefit package. A lip-service show of gratitude.

Gratitude.

Malcolm Mitchell didn't know the meaning of it.

David's focus slipped. In a split second, almost too late, the road ahead seemed to disappear.

The Accord swerved out of David's control. The road bent sharply to the left without warning. The car lunged into it in an overconfident lurch before David could react. His hands tighter on the steering wheel than ever, he yanked hard to the left, trying to force the car to *please, please, please* make the turn. Ahead, where the ongoing path of the straight would have been, was a low barrier; black and white chevrons tried to flash out the warning that this was a bend, that he should drop his speed, take heed, slow slow slow down.

Shit, shit, shit.

The back end of the car pulled out to the right as David fought to regain control. His foot pumped the brake as somehow he drew on fragments of memory.

Pump don't slam. Keep it together. It's going to be okay. It's going to be okay.

After the night he'd had, there was a vein of dark inevitability mixed into David's frantic panic. Wouldn't it be the perfect ending to the shitshow of a day to career off into the blackness?

Amanda, a widow. She would suit the role. He could almost imagine her shopping for her funeral dress. What an occasion. What an excuse.

Lottie, though.

She wouldn't notice I was gone.

Perhaps there was a case for him to stop fighting, to let the speed take him. Go with the flow.

The thoughts as dark as the moonless night flooded his head, but despite himself, he tugged at the steering wheel, wrestling it into submission.

David's heart jack hammered in his chest as the car began to respond.

Not tonight. Not like this.

His biceps ached with tension, and as the car gradually came back under his control, he let his arms relax, but not completely.

He had to carry on. He had to keep moving. He had to focus.

Even though the road ahead was straight, the surface was slick with the ongoing torrential rain, mirroring his headlights like moonlight on a lake. There was danger everywhere on a journey like this. He couldn't afford to romanticise the scene or underestimate the need for caution.

Equally, this was no time to surrender to his darker thoughts.

Level head. Focus. Onwards.

Releasing one hand from the steering wheel, David pulled a cloth from the side of his door and wiped at his brow. It was meant for cleaning or clearing the window rather than for personal hygiene, but it hadn't been used, and he needed it now. Sweat was beading on his forehead, and it felt grotesque. He needed it gone. Lottie would do that thing where she pretended to gag - as she seemed to do so often these days - but she wasn't here to see him. He could do whatever he wanted without the constant judgement of his wife and daughter. All he wanted to do was drive. Drive and get away. Somewhere. Anywhere.

The route hair-pinned to the left, but now David was in control, focussed on the road ahead. Everything else was a distraction that he could push to the back of his mind. He didn't need to think about Amanda or Lottie, Mitchell or Johnson or…

He didn't need to think about it, so he didn't.

David came smoothly out of the last of another short series of bends and finally felt confident to apply gentle pressure to the accelerator. The road now was straight as far as his eye could see, but that wasn't far. Despite the efforts of his wipers, the rain was persistent, and his vision was severely limited. With every swipe, the windscreen was clear for a brief moment before the shimmer of rain obliterated his vision.

David reached down to his side, where his insulated mug usually rested on his daily drives. There was nothing but dead space. He needed coffee; the jolt to bring him back to the moment, to help him focus. He didn't smoke and rarely touched alcohol, but David loved himself a heavy dose of caffeine.

He brought his disappointed, empty hand back to the wheel and slapped it down again. Even though he wanted more than anything to keep moving, to never stop, his mind was already acting like a Google Map of where the nearest rest stop was. He wanted – no, he *needed* – a fix.

You're wired enough, he told himself, this time speaking the words out into the artificially heated air.

Either his wife or his daughter, he had no idea which, had stuck a vanilla cupcake air-freshener onto the vent on the passenger side. It made the inside of his car smell like a cheap, chemically fuelled bakery. Without coffee, the cloying sweetness was sticking to the back of his throat. He wanted to reach over, rip the yellow pod from his dash, and throw it out of the window.

Somehow, the smell made him crave his caffeine fix even more.

There's a truck stop.

Could be open.

Should be open.

It would be safe to stop there, get an Americano - hell, maybe an espresso on the side - fill the tank, and work out where the hell he was going to –

His thoughts were cut short.

Ahead.

By the roadside.

There was a shape.

His headlights caught onto it; just a suggestion of something other than trees space trees trees space.

At first, he thought it was a deer, young, spindly, separated from its herd. About the right size, maybe. He wasn't sure. The darkness, the shadows, and the constant downpour of rain made it hard to determine if there was anything there at all.

There were signs all along the road, that red triangle with the black stag. His foot automatically fell onto the brake pedal, slowing, cautious now.

Details became clearer as he approached, and drawing closer, it became obvious that it wasn't a deer at all: it was a person.

It was a short, slim person.

A short, slim person wearing a thin hooded jacket and jeans.

A girl. It looked like a girl.

Only the person's frame gave him cause to assume their gender. The figure was slight. If he hadn't had his headlights switched to full beam, he might have missed her altogether. There was no natural light to the side of the road, only the skeletal overhang of trees.

A girl. Not a deer, not a danger, just a skinny little girl.

How had she found her way out here?

No streetlights. The only light came from David's speeding car; the sky was merely a storm-muffled backdrop.

No bus stops, not on this route. He hadn't passed a car. He thought again. He hadn't seen another car since he'd left Maplewood. He hadn't seen that bend that almost wiped him out. Had he been paying that little attention to the environment that he had missed a damn car?

It was possible.

But he couldn't stop. Tonight was not the night for heroics. Tonight was the night for moving onwards, getting his coffee, getting away, away, away.

In the time it took to have these thoughts, David had approached the girl and passed her. He couldn't stop himself from casting a look in her direction as they briefly drew level. Momentarily, she glowed like an angel in the light reflected on her pale face. There was no time to make out anything other than desperation.

Shit, shit, shit. Not tonight. Not tonight.

Nothing good could come of this.

Still driven by an uncontrollable impulse, David slowed to a drowsy crawl.

Aiming his gaze at the rear-view mirror, David could still make out the shape of the girl through the rain blurred back window. She was standing in the road, now, waving her arms in a gesture that reminded him of the star jumps that Lottie had loved performing as a kid.

He had driven past, but she had not given up hope. How long had she been on this road? How many cars had passed her by?

The thought of his daughter caused his foot to drop further on the brake pedal. What if it was Lottie out here? What if she was alone and desperate on the forest road? The digital display on his dash said that it was past midnight. Too late for anyone to be here.

It wasn't just a girl out there; it was someone's daughter.

Shit!

David brought the car to a stop and slammed his hands furiously on the steering wheel. A part of him knew he was about to make a terrible decision, but once he had personified the figure by the road, he had no alternative other than to pick her up.

He threw the car into reverse, the white lights at the back of his vehicle creating a ghostly path on the tarmac as he slowly approached the figure. The road was empty apart from the two of them.

Seeing David's change of heart, the girl had started running along the muddy, thin track that laced the roadside.

Don't slip, David thought, instinctively. *Wait now, I'm coming.*

His paternal instinct fought with his survival instinct for control, and the former was winning.

As he skidded to a stop beside the sodden figure, the girl darted towards the vehicle, hood pulled up high around her face and bag slung over her shoulder. David pressed the lock release button, and the girl pulled open the door.

He didn't know what to say. What was the appropriate etiquette when picking up a stranger in the middle of the night?

"I'm sorry," he said.

The thought of driving past her, making her wait, making her stand in the rain for those additional minutes somehow came to the forefront of his mind.

"You need a ride?"

He wanted to take the words back as soon as they came out. Of course she wanted a ride. Was making himself look like an idiot going to make her feel any safer? Perhaps it didn't matter.

"Thanks," she said. Her voice was fragile, birdlike.

She girl clambered into the car, throwing her bag into the footwell, settling her legs into position around it as she shuffled in the seat. Her breath puffed cloud-like in the warm air.

Looking across at her, David's stomach wrenched with the sudden realisation that he had just let a complete stranger become his passenger. He had taken on a responsibility that he definitely did not need. Tonight, of all nights, he had picked up a potential problem.

It was too late now.

The wind slammed the door shut behind her and She was in.

The smell of wet wool, rain, and something else, more earthy, filled the space. David tried not to breathe too deeply as he pulled off and accelerated down the road.

"I-I'm so grateful," the girl spluttered, her voice shaking from the cold. "My car broke down almost an hour ago. I was giving up hope."

"Okay," David said, not knowing quite what the right response should be. "Did you want to go back? See if I can give you a hand with it?"

"Uh…" The girl hesitated.

"I don't know why I said that," David sighed. "I know exactly nothing about cars. Where did you leave it? Is it safe?"

The girl nodded.

"Yeah," she said.

"I must have driven past it," David said, with a frown. "I don't remember seeing anything."

The girl shrugged.

"I've been walking for half that time, I guess. It's not far back."

David raised his eyebrows. He'd had a lot to think about. It was possible.

He changed tack. "Did you try phoning…"

"My mobile…I couldn't get a signal out here," she said. "If I can get a lift with you, I'll get someone to come out and meet me. Is there a rest stop? I don't…I don't really know this road."

David reached into his pocket and pulled out his own phone. He already knew, though, that there would be no connection here. He'd driven this road enough times. There would be no signal until they broke the other side of the hills.

They were alone.

He shook his head in apology.

"There's a place about thirty miles ahead," he said. "You might be able to make a call from there. There used to be a pay phone."

He shot her a look, wondering if she was even aware what he was talking about. He knew from interactions with his daughter that things he took for granted as common knowledge were less common now than he imagined.

The girl's expression gave no reaction.

"I was planning on stopping anyway." He tried to give her a reassuring smile without looking too creepy. "Where are you heading?"

The girl paused for a moment too long.

"Anywhere warm and dry is good enough for me," she said with a smile that looked forced and nervous.

The vagueness of the girl's response made David furrow his brow, but he quickly gathered himself.

He thought for a split second that his question shouldn't have been *where* are *you heading?* but *where* were *you heading?*. People didn't take this road unless they were going somewhere. Warm and dry *wasn't* good enough.

Perhaps she too was running from somewhere, not towards anything specific.

And he hadn't seen a car, had he?

Her night couldn't have been any worse than his, though. She hadn't done what he had.

The thought caused a ball to form in his throat, and he coughed, trying to force it out.

He wasn't going to start asking questions. The girl might have some of her own.

"You okay?" she asked, almost apologetically.

David nodded, without looking at her.

He was far from okay.

Pressing his foot more heavily on the accelerator, David hoped beyond hope that he'd made the right decision when he stopped to pick up the girl.

Tonight, there was too much at stake. The last thing he needed was to add another variable into the mix. The last thing he needed was anyone finding out what he had done.

TWO

David Five Hours Ago

David stared intently into the mirror, looking himself dead in the eyes. This was it. This was finally it.

Eleven years in the company, rising through the ranks.

Eleven years of overtime, with long hours and fewer holidays than he was supposedly entitled to.

Eleven years, all for this.

Tonight was the night that he would finally receive the recognition for everything he had done.

"Thank you," he said.

No, that wasn't it. That wasn't the right tone.

He cleared his throat and spoke again.

"It's been a long journey," he said, and again cut himself short.

No one cares.

No one cares what it's taken to win this award.

Forty-five years old. The grey hairs had taken root a decade ago, and despite his wife's pleas for him to take to the dye, he had rolled with the punches, embraced the aging process. It was easier for men, but she had always been one for appearances. Hers remained immaculate, but he wasn't so bad, was he?

He was tall, but wiry. If he had been a few inches shorter, he wouldn't have cut much of a figure. His slim face let the age show before its time.

David leaned closer to the mirror, scrutinising every wrinkle. His long hours at the office had no doubt contributed to the sagging bags beneath his eyes and had definitely not contributed to the so-called laughter lines. Still, here he was, alive, healthy, successful, and finally, *finally* about the receive the recognition – and healthy bonus – he deserved.

He raised an imaginary glass as if making a toast and watched his reflection form a smile that he didn't feel.

"Thanks…" he began again.

Off to his side, a deep, dirty laugh rang out from the doorway. David felt heat rush to his cheeks, and his reflection confirmed the red flush. He turned to look at Amanda as she walked into the room and glided towards him.

She was a true cliché of a wife: everything he had ever dreamed of in a woman. At least once a day, he wondered why she had stood by him through the years. More often, he wondered why she was even with him in the first place.

Not that he was all about what was on the surface. Amanda *had* stood by him. Whatever else had happened between them, she had been solid. She had been there.

"You didn't write a speech already?" Amanda said, stopping behind him and putting her hands on his shoulders. She dug her fingertips into his muscles, and he let them sink at her touch.

She was good, so good.

For a moment, he thought of spinning around, grabbing hold of her and taking her to their bed. How long had it been? Too long, that was all he knew. They had settled into a routine of sleeping when it pleased them and pleasing themselves while the other slept.

There was time, though, tonight, wasn't there?

David felt his hands tremble. Amanda wouldn't. Not with their daughter in the house.

Instead, he shook his head and carried on as though the thoughts had never entered his head.

"No," David replied, his voice tinged with an attempt at lightness despite his crippling anxiety. "Just practicing how not to make a fool of myself,"

Amanda's eyes, warm with a mix of amusement and understanding, met his.

"You'll be great," she assured him, her voice steady and sure. "You've earned this, David. Everyone knows it."

"I didn't…" David began but couldn't finish the sentence. He didn't want to give voice to his deepest fear.

"Didn't what?" Amanda said, tilting her head.

David sighed heavily. "I didn't want to prepare something, write something, in case. Well, you know."

Amanda shook her head. She was going to make him say it.

"In case," he said, lowering his voice as he stumbled over the words he was loath to say, "I don't get it."

Amanda's mouth formed a tiny 'o' and then she let out a high-pitched laugh that made David shudder.

"Of course you'll get it," she said, in a way that made him feel stupid rather than reassured.

"Nothing is ever a foregone conclusion," David said.

"You're *guaranteed* to get it," Amanda smiled, reaching out towards him.

David stopped her hand mid-air, grabbing her wrist slightly tighter than he had planned. She tried to conceal the wince as she pulled away, but not quickly enough to disguise her pain.

His apology crumbled in his mouth; it wouldn't mean anything. Instead, he pursed his lips and withdrew his grip.

"Don't," he said. "Don't say that."

"What?" she laughed. "You think I'll jinx it for you?" There was an icy undertone to her words.

"I'm sorry," he said, nodding towards her arm. "I was just…I mean…look, I'm sorry."

"Yeah, whatever," Amanda said. "Perhaps you should just go on your own?"

It was David's turn to try - and fail - to cover his emotions. He looked at his wife with unveiled disappointment, and, with a gulp, he shook his head.

"Amanda, no," He heard the desperation in his voice and tried to moderate it as he continued. "I need you with me. All the other wives will be there."

"*All the other wives*," she echoed. "Tag-a-longs. Cheerleaders." She spoke the last word as though it tasted bad.

"That's not what I meant," David said, averting his eyes.

When Amanda got like this, there was no point trying to reason with her. He had hurt her, even though it was unintentional, and now he was going to receive his punishment.

"I would really like you to be with me," he said, in a last-ditch attempt to sway her.

She had ironed his shirt, laid out his tux, hell she'd even picked out fresh socks and briefs so he could change out of the ones he had worn all day in the office.

And, of course, she had done so much more.

That line about there being a great woman behind every great man was true in his case, but what they didn't mention was that the great woman could also be a moody bitch.

When he and Amanda met, she was a personal shopper, a job that seemed her destined calling. Helping others spend their money had always come naturally to her, combining her keen eye for style with her magnetic personality. She thrived in the vibrant bustle of upscale boutiques and luxury department stores, where she curated wardrobes for the city's elite. Her clients adored her not only for her impeccable taste but also for her ability to make each of them feel like the most important person in the room. Her days were a whirlwind of silk and cashmere, espresso meetings, and whispered confidences in plush fitting rooms.

Whilst Amanda was in the midst of this glamorous career. David, on the other hand, was a rising figure in corporate sales, a world away from the dazzling fashion circles Amanda frequented. That was before he ever heard of Tursten Mitchell, let alone devoted his working life to them.

Their meeting was almost cinematic, taking place at a crowded charity auction that Amanda attended with a client. David was there to secure a deal with potential business partners, but his focus shifted the moment he saw Amanda. She was negotiating over a piece of art, her expression one of concentrated charm. Intrigued by her confidence and allure, David found himself drawn to her. He was captivated not just by her beauty but by her vivacious spirit and the passionate way she engaged with the world around her. It was a meeting of two different worlds, but between them sparked an undeniable connection that neither could ignore.

She had taken time off when their daughter was born and somehow never went back to the life she had before.

Not that motherhood suited her, more that being the head of a family did. At home, Amanda was in charge, and what she said usually went.

Now she gave David a cool look.

He knew he wasn't going to be able to change her mind.

"Lottie wanted me to stay home with her anyway," Amanda said, as though the matter had already been decided. Perhaps it had. The whole getting-angry-over-nothing-as-a-way-out was a ruse she had used before.

Amanda had her ways, and David had no ways around them.

He nodded his head, just once, slowly, in acknowledgement.

"Something special?" he asked, although the answer would be unimportant.

Amanda waved her hand, as though brushing away a fly, and took a step back, away from him, towards the door.

He had to let her go.

Again, he nodded. There was no point pushing the conversation further. There was no point in him trying to get what he wanted for once. No point at all.

What Lottie wanted; Lottie got.

What Amanda wanted; Amanda got.

"We'll get takeout and have a girls' night," Amanda beamed, as though it was a new idea that had just occurred to her. As though it wasn't what she had wanted all along.

"Okay," David smiled, hoping it looked genuine. "Take my card," he said, digging his wallet out of his back pocket and pulling out his plastic. "I won't need it tonight. Get whatever you two want."

Amanda beamed and pulled her hands up to her chest in an over-reaction of excitement.

"Thanks, honey," she said.

David managed a swift nod in response and put his wallet down next to him on the bed, clearing his hands to offer a hug; it was too late. Amanda had turned heel and hurried out of the room, no doubt to share the good news with their daughter.

David was left alone again, and with only his reflection for company, the room was filled with an uncomfortable silence. The weight of his unease settled heavily in his chest as he stared at his own face in the mirror once more. His expression, once confident and composed, was now strained and haunted.

Was there any point going to the ceremony alone? Winning the award meant nothing to him without recognition from Amanda.

The thought was jarring. Was that what he had been working for? All these years, just to prove something to his wife. Something that she should already have known.

The Tursten-Mitchell Alpha Achievement Award was the big one. Once a decade - only every ten years – a single employee was chosen to receive the prestigious plaque and the £10k cheque that came with it. He doubted, now, that there would be an actual cheque. The previous winner was probably the last to receive that outdated payment method, although the £10k was no doubt worth a damn sight more then than today.

It wasn't about the money, though. Not really.

If it wasn't for the money and it wasn't for Amanda, why was he so amped for the award?

Johnson. He knew it was because of Michael Johnson.

The thought of his coworker's name sparked a fierce competitive fire within him, a smouldering ember that had driven him through countless late nights and early mornings. Johnson, always the golden boy of the office, with his easy charm and seemingly effortless success, had been David's nemesis since he joined the company. Three years he had been there. Only three years, and yet in the back of David's mind, lingered the ever-present threat that Johnson could be the one to lift the plaque.

Because of Johnson, David had pushed himself harder, determined to prove not just to Amanda, but to everyone, that he was the better man. And at what cost? The nights he could have spent with Amanda and Charlotte, the moments of joy he had sacrificed on the altar of ambition—they seemed like a steep price for a victory that was not yet assured.

A surge of defiance rose within him, a refusal to let this moment define him. Yes, he would go to the ceremony.

Not for Amanda. Not for the money. Certainly not for Johnson. He would go for himself.

To stand on that stage and accept the Tursten-Mitchell Alpha Achievement Award as a testament to his own dedication, his own sacrifices. It would be a moment to acknowledge his hard work, yes, but also a moment to reflect on what truly mattered.

Tonight, David was finally going to get what he deserved.

Tonight, nothing could go wrong.

He wouldn't let it.

THREE

Emma Five Hours Ago

Emma reached out and rubbed at a smudge of foundation on her vanity mirror. Whatever she did, however often she cleaned it, there was always something left behind. She looped the end of her sweatshirt over her forefinger and went at it again until the beige stain transferred onto the sleeve.

One of the bulbs at the side of the mirror was out; a black space punctuated the border around her reflected image. The desktop was covered in a scattered assortment of makeup palettes and discarded brushes. Among them were a plethora of false eyelashes, some in cases, some loose, sticking like caterpillars to the grimy varnished wood. In three of the four mugs she had gathered, a furry blue film had formed on top of the remnants of abandoned long dead instant coffee. She paid rent; what happened in her room was on her.

Still, as she looked at her reflection, all she could see was disappointment.

Her sandy blonde hair, once a subject of envy between her and her sister, was pulled back into a messy bun, greasy strands escaping at the sides. A red pimple was starting to show itself on her sallow left cheek, and she ran her finger over it, feeling the tension in her skin. The high cheekbones she had always loved were now sharp and defined, a result of losing too much weight. She barely ate, and her gym classes had sometimes been the only way she could clear her mind. The two didn't sit well together.

It had been a challenging year, and her appearance echoed that struggle—her eyes, once bright and lively, now appeared dimmed under the persistent weight of insomnia.

The room around her, once a haven of warmth and laughter, mirrored her inner turmoil. The walls, adorned with faded posters of rock bands and movie stars, seemed to loom over her, the colours more muted than she remembered. Clothes lay strewn across a chair, each piece discarded after a hopeful yet fruitless attempt to find something that felt right. The air felt stagnant, thick with the scent of old perfume and the ghost of incense burned during better days.

As Emma turned away from her tarnished reflection, her gaze fell upon the small pile of unopened letters and bills that had accumulated at the corner of her desk. Each envelope was a reminder of the outside world's demands that she felt increasingly incapable of meeting. The room now felt more like a prison than a sanctuary.

Gone were the days of college and carefree living. Now, all that remained was this small, dingy room and the broken girl staring back at her. Emma grabbed a small glass dispenser and pumped out a blob of foundation onto her fingers.

It used to match her healthy complexion perfectly, but now it only served as a reminder of what she had lost. The make-up was a healthy light tan colour; her skin was pale, wan.

With sudden anger, Emma shoved her hand towards the mirror and swiped a thick layer across its surface, rubbing until her reflection disappeared. The pressure in her chest grew as she continued to obliterate any trace of herself in the mirror. Tears streamed down her face as she gasped for air, each sob shaking her body uncontrollably.

Finally, she stopped, her arm aching, and the mirror covered in a sepia-coloured film. Emma knew that the person she used to be would have found it artistic, but the person she was today only felt pain and self-loathing. She collapsed onto her bed, letting out deep, shuddering sobs.

As she released her emotions, a familiar pain took hold. Her temples throbbed in sync with the steady beat of her heart, each pulsation feeling like a hammer against her skull.

Once the migraines had come with alarming regularity. Now, they had become polite enough to wait for a trigger before flooring her.

They had mocked her monthly menstrual cycle before her periods stopped. Every twenty-eight days, as soon as her hormones had kicked in, so had the vice-like headaches. The bleeding had stopped, and the migraines had nothing to cling to. The excessive weight loss she had suffered had been good for something, at least.

Today, it was the thick, heavy air presaging a storm that was rolling out the red carpet for her migraine. She knew the bad weather was coming, even before she saw the dark clouds and ominous shadows. And just as the first rumble of thunder sounded, her internal barometer was proven infallible once again.

Emma pressed the heels of her hands into her forehead, fighting back against the tension in her pressure points.

"Not tonight," she said in a low growl. *"Not tonight."*

The girl pulled open the top drawer on the vanity, sweeping her hand around through various bottles and brushes, the debris of her so-called beauty routine. Not knowing where her meds were was a good sign. It meant it had been a long time since the pain had visited. No consolation now, though, as the migraine dug its claws into her.

Come on.

Come on.

Come on.

She repeated the phrase as she fell to her knees beside the unit and searched for the small round bottle that held her pain relief. She tugged out paracetamol and naproxen; they would do as half-measures, the hors d'oeuvres to the treatment she was looking for. Popping two of each from the blister packs into her sweaty palm, her eyes scanned the cluttered room for something to wash them down.

Grimacing again at the sight of the mugs, she grabbed a bottle of cola from on the floor by her bed. It hadn't been there more than a few days; it would be fine. She sloshed the tablets down and went back to her search for the triptans.

"I'm fine, by the way," she shouted, flinching at the sound of her own voice. "Don't worry about me."

Every noise she made thudded against her skull. *Where the...*

Emma could feel the frustration mingling with the pain coursing through her body. It was building like a toddler's tantrum; she was on the verge of ripping out the drawer and tipping its contents onto her bed. It wasn't as though it would make her room any untidier.

Just as she felt the strung-out tension of her mood was about to reach breaking point, her fingers closed around the small white bottle.

Yes. Yes, yes, yes.

Emma let out a long, slow breath that she had been unconsciously holding and worked her fingers on popping the cap. There was a simple arrow to line up, but as tense as she was, every controlled movement was a Herculean effort.

Slay the Minotaur, clean the crappy stables, open the medicine bottle.

With one final push, Emma slid the lid free and looked down into the bottle. There were four tablets left, and she needed two – at least two – right then. There was no time to write a reminder to order more. She needed the pain in her head to stop. The triptans were good, but they would take twenty minutes to work, and she wanted to start that countdown as soon as possible.

Not bothering with the cola this time, she dry-swallowed two of the pills and let herself fall back onto the bed. Reaching a hand to the plug socket, Emma plunged the room into darkness and lay silent, waiting for the medication to take hold.

With her eyes closed, the silence of the flat enveloped Emma. She had grown accustomed to the constant presence of the tinny speaker on her smart device, shuffling the playlist that she and Angeline had been curating since they decided to split the cost of a music streaming subscription. They didn't always agree on every track, but there was enough crossover to keep both of them happy.

The thought brought a smile to Emma's lips as the pain began to subside. Wasn't that how it was in their relationship with each other, too? Sisters, two years apart. It could have gone one way or the other.

Although they had certainly had their moments over the years, the arguments that seemed so intense at the time had melted into nothing. Using each other's make-up, borrowing clothes without asking, all of their little niggles were in the past.

They learned to share everything, saw their matching tattoos as a symbol of their strength rather than imitation. Without each other, they were nothing.

She tugged up her sleeve and looked at the text, etched on her flesh in courier font.

Everything happens for a reason.

The words swam in the intoxication from the mix of painkillers and the dull residual throb at her temples.

Emma covered them up.

"Just so you know, I'm rocking your sweatshirt," she said, not loud enough for her sister to hear.

She rolled onto her side, pulled the hood up over her head, letting it flop across her eyes, blocking out the dim room around her, inhaling Angeline's scent.

Twenty, perhaps twenty-five minutes later, long enough for the pain to subside, Emma snapped into consciousness and sat bolt upright with a juddering sob.

"Angeline," she shouted, but there was no response.

Emma rolled her eyes, pulled the hood away from her face, and checked the time glowing on her alarm clock.

She hadn't been out of it for long, but still she felt as though she had woken from a deep but unsatisfying sleep.

Emma clicked the switch to turn on the lamp on her vanity, screwing her eyes tightly just in case the brightness was too sharp in her fragile state.

Fine. It was fine.

Tentatively, she relaxed her eyes.

Still, she was groggy. Her mouth was dry, her tongue unnaturally large, with a foul salty taste she had to wash away. Her arm thrashed out towards the cola bottle again, but she thought better of it. She needed water.

She needed vodka.

"Come on," she muttered. "Come on."

Emma reached out for the bag at the end of her bed and clicked open the fastener. Purse. Keys. Charger. Her eyes fell upon something else, and she pulled it out, sticking it into her pocket instead. Her fingers touched plastic, and she drew out the water bottle, giving it a shake before unscrewing the lid. There was enough.

Downing what was left of the liquid inside, she made a mental note to refill it.

Stay hydrated.

She heard Angeline's voice.

Emma sighed. The best way to combat migraines was to try to prevent them from happening in the first place. Drinking enough water, getting enough sleep, minimising stress. But that wasn't the world Emma lived in.

Confident that she was over the worst of the attack, Emma snatched her mobile from the edge of her desk and made a call.

"It's me," she said. "Again." She paused before continuing. "Look, I can't sit here all night. I'm going nuts on my own. I'm going to do it. Tonight. I'm going now."

She didn't need to say anything else. She had already made up her mind.

Without hesitating, she clicked the red phone icon on her screen to end the call. She didn't want to be talked out of the decision that had taken her so long to make.

Emma pulled herself out of bed. It was more difficult than it should have been, but the sleep haze and the aftermath of the migraine fuzz slowed her down. She slid her phone into the back pocket of her jeans and clicked the clasp on her bag closed again.

With a wet wipe, she cleared a patch on her mirror and peered at herself one last time. There was a black smudge beneath her right eye, and she rubbed at it until it vanished. There was no need for make-up. There was no need to brush her hair. No need for anything. Not for where she was heading.

Stepping out of her room into the hallway, Emma paused. She grabbed her coat from the hook and pulled it on.

"I'm going out," she called. "Don't wait up."

With that, she zipped her puffer jacket and slipped her hood up onto her head. The rain was going to last all night; she was going to need it.

FOUR

Now

The silence in the car surrounded the travellers like bubble wrap. They had travelled for twenty minutes since the hitchhiker had climbed into the passenger seat. The rest stop was another twenty minutes ahead, given the driving conditions and the fact that David's earlier brush with the road had scared him enough to make him drive like his grandmother.

David stared ahead, directing his focus on the road, trying to decide whether he should speak.

Beside him, the girl fidgeted in her seat. She had thrown her bag down into the footwell, and now she was edging it gradually into a position that made it possible for her to stretch her short legs.

"Move it back if you want," David said. "There's a lever…"

But the girl had already reached down and pushed the metal bar to allow her to slide backwards, extending the leg room. The seat threw her further than she intended, but she remained straight-faced.

"Thanks," she said, giving her bag a last shove so that it was just out of reach of her tiptoes.

The only passengers David usually carried were Amanda and Charlotte; neither of them needed much space, and neither spent long enough in the car with him to bother making any adjustments. Amanda would rather call a cab than ask him to pick her up; Lottie frequently told him she would rather die than be seen in his car, but that teenage hyperbole seemed to fall by the wayside when she was desperate for a lift.

He couldn't imagine his daughter getting into a vehicle with a stranger anywhere, never mind at midnight in the middle of nowhere.

He didn't want to think about it.

But here he was.

The girl was in his car.

She was someone's daughter, too.

If this was Charlotte, how would he want the driver to behave?

He would probably want them to phone him and tell him that his child was trying to catch a lift from anyone that passed by. He would want them to call him instead, so he could pick her up himself. Had something happened to her? Something more than the car breakdown she claimed had left her out here.

And if she was seeking help, wouldn't she be heading towards town rather than away from it?

All that lay ahead was forest, moorland, and the truck stop that he hoped was still open so he could get the petrol and coffee he so desperately needed.

David stole a quick look at his front seat passenger. He was being hypersensitive, and he knew it; he didn't want to do anything that would make her uncomfortable. He couldn't ask any more questions. It was none of his business.

He didn't want to ask too many questions, but maybe more than that, he didn't want to answer any.

At the back of his mind was another thought, more insidious. He didn't want to embarrass himself.

A smell of damp forest had entered the car with the girl. It was almost as though she hadn't simply been walking along the road but had come from out there in the trees. He couldn't see her shoes, boots, trainers, whatever she was wearing on her feet, but mud wouldn't give him any further clues anyway. Her hood was still pulled up over her hair, but dark blonde strands escaped at the sides, dry-clinging to her face. He had a sudden urge to reach across and brush the errant hairs away from her skin, but even Lottie would protest if he followed his paternal instincts.

If this was his daughter...

If this was Charlotte...

If this was his daughter, she would never be out here in the rain, in the dark, in a stranger's car. For that, he was grateful.

Dear uneventful Charlotte. Glued to her phone. The benefits of raising an internet-addicted bedroom dweller were starting to become clear to him.

David turned his attention back in their direction of travel. Nothing changed ahead of them. The scenery beside the road may as well have been a zoetrope, an endless repeating loop. The wipers continued their futile attempt at clearing the windscreen, and the world beyond remained an uncertain blur.

He couldn't stay silent. Not with the girl in the car. He had to say something. He had to fill the awkward emptiness.

Silence had been fine when he was on his own, but now, with the girl here, it seemed more appropriate to have some kind of noise in the car.

"You want to listen to the radio? Some Taylor Swift or something. That what you kids are into now?" David reached towards the radio.

"I'm not a kid. I'm twenty-one, sir."

"And I'm not a sir. I'm David."

The girl flicked her eyes across at him. He glanced quickly in her direction and then turned his gaze back to the night ahead of them, the blackness split by headlights and the trees, the endless trees.

"It's hard to tell with kids…with young people these days," David said. "You look around the same age as my daughter. She just turned nineteen and she…" He cut himself off.

He didn't want to talk about Charlotte. There was no need to discuss anything personal with this stranger. That was the whole point of turning the radio on. He didn't want silence, but he didn't want to share his life story either.

Twenty-one though.

This girl. The way she had got into the car, the way she sat, the way she spoke to him. It seemed a world away from what he knew of his daughter.

Silence hung in the air for longer than David was comfortable with. He had to speak.

"You have a name, Twenty-One?" he asked, trying to inject a tone of friendly banter into the question.

"Angeline," she said.

"Right," David said, with a hint of surprise. "That's a different one." He hadn't intended to ask any further questions. He didn't want to make a friend. He just didn't want the girl to feel uncomfortable. "Does it..." He paused mid-question before continuing. "Does it mean anything?"

The girl shrugged. "Probably, sure." She sighed. "Listen, you can call me Twenty-One instead if you like. I think I prefer it."

David let out a short, dry laugh. The girl was finding her balls. Maybe there was more to her than the quiet voice and endless fidgeting after all.

"How about we just stop asking each other questions and I put the radio on, hmm?"

The girl nodded, but seeing his eyes were still trained on the road, she vocalised her agreement.

"Sounds good," she said. "David."

45

The word, his name, sounded strange coming from her mouth. He wasn't used to talking to kids. Young people. All Charlotte's friends existed outside of his sphere of interaction with her. They were people she knew at school – at college now. Where had the time gone? – or online. There were some youngsters in the company, sure, but they called him Mister Burnham, or, as Miss Twenty-One had tried, *Sir*.

When the radio burst into life, it was the sound of an unidentifiable indie pop band. Not Taylor Swift, but that was as much as David knew.

He looked over towards the girl to gauge her reaction, but there was none. She was tapping at her phone screen.

"You got a signal?" he asked.

The girl made a *hmm* sound, before looking back at him and waving the handset.

"Out here?" she said. "Seems unlikely, David."

The way she said his name made the sentence sound sarcastic and bitter, or perhaps he was so used to hearing it used that way that his mind leapt at that interpretation of tone. She was defrosting, that was for sure.

Who even used his name now? Amanda. Malcolm. Michael.

He felt bile rise in his throat and swallowed hard.

"What is it?" he asked, to distract himself from his thoughts more than from any genuine interest.

On closer inspection, not that he could look too closely as he drove, David could see the telltale brick shapes of a Tetris-style game on the small bright screen.

The girl looked at him, and gestured towards the road, as though he needed to be reminded to look where he was going instead of studying her phone.

"Used to play that when I was a kid," he said, and again snapped his mouth shut. She wasn't a kid. She was twenty-one. He was being patronising. Annoying. Everything his daughter always accused him of. Everything Amanda...

He pursed his lips and decided that less was more. He should stop talking. Let the radio fill the blank space.

But the girl made another small noise, like a laugh. It didn't sound unkind.

"It's a classic," she said, not taking her eyes off the screen.

The song on the radio had finished playing in the background while they stumbled through their conversation. Instead, now, there was a woman's voice. A local accent for local radio, none of that Radio Four received pronunciation bullshit.

"...the discovery of a woman's body in a shallow grave in forest off the A617 near Maplewood."

David's arm jerked instinctively towards the radio, hitting the power off button.

"Taylor Swift might come on next," the girl deadpanned, pressing her finger on top of his, bringing the radio back to life.

The feeling of her skin on his was the opposite of comforting. He froze, listening to the words as the newsreader continued.

"...a local couple walking their dog, who immediately contacted the police."

David slowed the car slightly as he looked over at her. She was staring at the radio, their hands still touching over the power switch, as though it were a person in the car with them, talking directly to her.

"That's not far from..." David began to speak, and she shushed him, withdrawing her hand and batting at him.

The announcer, herself a young-sounding female presenter, continued. Her voice wavered as she spoke, in a way her professionalism couldn't mask.

"The identity of the woman, as well as the circumstances leading to her death, remains unclear at this early stage."

"Police are urging anyone with information, no matter how insignificant it may seem, to come forward."

"We will continue to provide updates on this developing story as more details become available."

It was only then, when the broadcaster moved on to the weather, that the girl finally spoke.

"Looks like it's lucky you picked me up," she said.

David's response was a non-committal grunt. He wished he could feel the relief or satisfaction a good deed was supposed to deliver, but all he felt was the tightening noose of circumstance around his neck.

The silence between them that followed her remark was thick and laced with tension. The girl's casual comment about luck only deepened his disquiet. In the background, another nondescript vocalist sang a cover version of a track David recognised, but he thought better of mentioning it. He let the radio fill the space between them, hoping there were none of the updates or details that the announcer had promised.

He didn't want to hear them.

The news was too close to home.

The car's interior felt increasingly claustrophobic as the road stretched endlessly before them.

He glanced sideways at the hitchhiker; her face was partially obscured by the hood of her jacket. She seemed to be lost in thought, gazing out of the window into the night. He considered asking her more about where she was going, but hesitated, the words catching in his throat.

Instead, David tried to focus on the road, but his mind kept wandering back to the girl beside him. She had appeared out of nowhere, and now they were travelling together, bound by a shared destination yet separated by a gulf of unknowns.

David's thoughts raced, replaying the moment he had seen her standing by the roadside. Had he made a mistake stopping for her? His gut twisted with foreboding, mingling with the rain's persistent drumming against the car.

Perhaps she *had* been lucky, but the night wasn't over yet. There was a storm to get through first.

FIVE

David Four Hours Ago

Despite his resolve to attend the ceremony alone, even when dressed and ready to go, David couldn't shake the gnawing feeling that something was off about Amanda's reluctance to join him. Sure, he had given her the excuse she needed, but the more he thought about it, the thinner it seemed. He'd held her arm, just a fraction too tightly, perhaps a second too long. He'd caught her too sharply, unawares, off-guard. Sure, whatever. All of that. He was guilty of whatever she wanted to throw at him.

He knew there was no point arguing, and she knew that *he* knew.

Their relationship had deteriorated into a perverse game of cat and mouse. She toyed with him until she tired of him, and he let it happen.

Time and again, he let it happen.

Hadn't she been there for him, though? Wasn't that exactly what he had been thinking before she walked into the bedroom and let him ruin his own evening?

It wasn't just the tension between him and Amanda on this particular evening that troubled him, although that was certainly a cause for concern. It was something deeper, buried beneath layers of pretence and denial. David had always prided himself on his intuition, his ability to read people and situations with uncanny precision. But lately, his instincts had been clouded by a growing sense of paranoia.

Something was off. Something beyond the here and now. David felt a warning buzz, like a Geiger's needle on the rise. If Amanda was about to go nuclear, he had to be prepared.

The best source of information in the house was their daughter. She picked up the tells he never could, and if she was feeling particularly snarky, she was more than happy to share them. He hoped it was one of those days.

There was no such thing as knocking in their home. If the bedroom door was closed, it was a sign to stay away, keep out. Of course, Amanda had left their daughter's room not long before David made his way along the landing. She could have been the one to leave the door ajar; the welcome may have been unintended. Still, he took his chance.

David paused, his palm sweaty against the wooden jamb. Charlotte was looking down at her phone screen, her face illuminated by its blue-tinged glow. There was no way of knowing whether the voice coming from the speaker was one of her friends or another of those mini sound bites she was obsessed with scrolling.

He had tried to keep up with the times. Everyone was on LinkedIn, of course, but all the Snaptoks and Tikchats had passed him by. Charlotte, though, was a screen swiping addict.

Once, a couple of years earlier, he had suggested to Amanda that they implement a 'no phones at the dinner table' rule. The result was that Charlotte had point blank refused to eat dinner with her parents from that point onwards. Even when Amanda relented – on the same evening – and tried to blame the whole regime shift on David, Lottie had dug in. Rather than improving communication within the family, it had been yet another brick of bitterness in the growing wall of resentment.

David was always the bad guy, and most of the time, to keep the peace, he let it slide.

Taking a breath, he stepped into his daughter's room.

"Hey," David said, trying to sound casual.

Lottie whipped her head around, not bothering to mask her displeasure.

"Daddy." Her voice was hollow and unwelcoming.

"The door was open," he gestured apologetically. "Anyway, I just wanted to see my number one girl before…"

"Mummy says you're buying us dinner," Lottie said, seeming to remember that David had done something she should be grateful for, and ameliorating her tone. "Can I pick whatever I want?"

"As long as Mummy agrees," David said. At nineteen, he thought his daughter should have been long over calling her parents by their juvenile sounding baby names, but Amanda encouraged it. David's opinions weren't worth pushing over such a trivial matter, so *Mummy* and *Daddy* stood.

"She won't," Charlotte pouted. "It'll be dim sum again. It's not fair. Every time it's those stupid little icky dumplings."

What wasn't fair was that David was paying for the two of them to have the most expensive take out his wife could find. What wasn't fair was that Amanda was staying at home with their daughter rather than attending the ceremony with him. No one was interested in hearing that, though.

David inhaled again, steadying himself. No need to lose his temper. No need to let his bitterness creep into his tone.

"I'm sure she's looking forward to spending some time with you, Lots. Won't it be nice to have a girls' night?"

Lottie's lips curled downwards. "She probably won't even stay home with me anyway."

David looked up, disarmed, snapping to attention.

"Why would you say that?" he asked.

Charlotte's face reddened, and she looked away.

"Lottie?"

She shrugged and said nothing.

"Why would you say that?" he repeated, trying to keep his voice calm and non-accusatory.

Charlotte paused for a moment too long, her gaze focussed on the corner of the room, away from her father.

"Lottie?" David reached out towards her, his hand cupping her chin and bringing it around, so she was facing him.

"Don't okay. I just think she has better things to do than have some mummy-daughter time with me."

"That's not a nice thing to say about your mother," he said, ignoring the truth of the words. "And it's not what you meant either, is it?"

Lottie snapped her hand back as though it was touching a hot plate and jerked her head away from David's touch.

"What do you want me to say, Dad?" she said, shuffling up the bed away from him and pulling her fleece cover over her body. "If you don't know what I mean, I shouldn't be the one to tell you. You're better off without her. Better off there, better off here, okay?"

"Charlotte! That's your mother you're talking about." He moved his hand in a shushing motion, not only to stop the conversation but also to protect against the subject hearing them. In a hushed tone, he asked, "What do you mean?"

Charlotte's phone beeped again. Once, twice. Incoming messages. Friends David never saw. He knew so little about her, really. He knew so little about his wife.

The girl dipped her head beneath the blanket, a move she always used to end conversations. It frustrated David at the best of times, and this was not the best of times. He could hear his daughter's fingers tapping at the phone's glass screen, muffled by the covers.

"Charlotte May Burnham, you…"

As soon as he heard the words coming out of his mouth, he knew he was heading in the wrong direction. Using her full name was taking a position, letting his feelings show – and there was no place for that in this household.

"I'm sorry, Lottie," he said, lowering his voice and dropping to sit on the bed next to his daughter.

She shuffled away from him in an almost instinctive move.

"Hey," David said. "I'm sorry, okay. I'm just…I'm sorry." Again, he almost voiced his disappointment, and again he knew not to bother.

Charlotte pulled down the cover slightly from over her face and peered from beneath the pink teddy fleece.

Her eyes studied his face, and she was wordless for what seemed like an eternity before she finally spoke, breaking the silence between them. In the background, her phone continued to beep.

"Are you sad, Daddy?"

"What?" David was caught off guard. "No. I'm fine, hon."

"I'm sorry Mummy isn't going with you. Okay?"

David nodded.

"You're going to be happier without her there."

David scanned his daughter's face, searching for meaning, but couldn't find it.

She ventured a tiny smile. "You know what Mum's like," she said. The playfulness of her tone was a thin disguise. "She would want to be the centre of attention." Lottie placed her own hand over her father's, holding it in place in a tender gesture.

Was that the kind of person who Charlotte was destined to grow into? Would she evolve to become a younger, more stable version of her mother? David hoped his daughter would pick up all of his and Amanda's positive traits and none of the negative, but that had to be wishful thinking.

"Well, she *is* a lot more interesting to look at," David smiled, instead of heading down the road to criticism.

Charlotte patted her father's hand. "Silly Daddy," she said.

He forced a smile.

"Anyway, at least she'll be here with you. She *will* be here," David said. He couldn't forget what Lottie had implied earlier. Then, as if a sudden thought had struck him, he asked, "You're not planning on going out anywhere, are you?"

Charlotte shook her head without skipping a beat.

"In this weather? With my hair?" she smiled. "I don't think so, Daddy."

"Okay. Well, I'm taking the car. I won't be drinking. If you need anything…"

"I'm staying home with Mum," Charlotte said. Her voice was even and reassuring. Almost too controlled.

David nodded.

"Okay, hon."

He knew he'd got lucky with Charlotte. She was a stay-at-home mummy's girl, not a rebellious teen tearaway. He knew the type. He'd seen them around town, hanging out in the park as he drove past after dark, ducking in and out of the shadows on the streets. He didn't know what the kids were into these days, but he had a feeling that none of it was any good. Charlotte was safe in her bedroom, with the phone full of friends and her overbearing mother to keep her in check.

Amanda, on the other hand…

David bent to kiss his daughter on the cheek, and she rose to wrap her arms around him in a tight, uncharacteristic embrace.

"Knock 'em dead, Daddy," she whispered into his ear.

"I'll try, sweetheart," he murmured. "I'll try."

As David prepared to leave, he couldn't help but feel the weight of years of accumulated grievances and misunderstandings pressing down on him. The house, once a symbol of their shared dreams, now felt like a mausoleum for their failed aspirations. Every picture on the wall, every piece of furniture, seemed to mock his failed attempts at rekindling the love that once bound them. The silence of the house was oppressive, heavy with things unsaid and affection withheld. The soft tick of the clock in the hallway echoed like a slow, steady reminder that time was slipping away, that perhaps it was too late to mend what had been broken.

Stepping into the hallway, David paused for a moment. The air was thick with the scent of Amanda's perfume and something else, something colder, less comforting. It was the smell of loneliness, of empty rooms and silent dinners. As he passed the mirror by the front door, he caught a glimpse of himself again. The reflection staring back at him was a man he barely recognised—a man worn out by the pretence, by the constant effort it took to appear whole when he felt so fragmented. In that fleeting moment, a surge of resentment washed over him, not just toward Amanda but toward himself for allowing things to get this bad.

At least soon he would have the recognition of the award, the recognition that at least not everything had been in vain.

"Knock 'em dead," he repeated to the man in the mirror.

He couldn't bring himself to smile again as he walked out of the door.

SIX

Emma Four Hours Ago

The café on the corner of the high street had once been a Coffee Express franchise. After the pandemic, the big chain had decided that three outlets within a hundred-meter radius were a superfluous use of their dwindling resources, and now the only branch was a hole-in-the-wall at the train station. Now, instead, there was Urban Grind, exuding the charm of what a fifty-year-old might imagine young people thought was cool. And yes, they thought the clientele still used that word.

The walls were tiled with an ambitious mosaic of artificial plant panels. Although probably meant as an attempt at Instagrammable metropolitan greenery, the foliage sucked the light from the room, making it feel claustrophobic rather than cosy. Even from afar, the leaves were too uniform in shape and styling to be real. Urban Grind wasn't fooling anybody.

Still, the coffee was excellent, and the staff had stayed on after the takeover. Emma was an expert at overlooking the negative in favour of the positive, and her ongoing loyalty to Urban Grind was a prime example of her doglike nature.

On the plus side, since the switch in ownership, the coffee shop was now table-service rather than stand-at-the-counter. That suited Emma just fine.

She slipped into the back room where she had a choice of six empty tables and sat on one of the banquettes against the wall.

"Let me hang your coat," the waitress said, hurrying over to her.

When it had been a Coffee Express, the waitresses had been baristas. The sandwiches had been pre-packed. Angeline had always been with her.

Emma shook her head.

"I'm not staying long, Vanessa," she said, but the woman was already lifting the wet, slippery fabric from Emma's shoulders, tugging the sleeves from her arms.

"You'll leave puddles everywhere," Vanessa said. "Someone will slip. We will be sued. I'll be out of a job again."

Emma managed a small laugh at Vanessa's ever-present melodrama.

"I suppose you'll be warning me next about the dangers of hypothermia and pneumonia if I don't hurry on home this instant," she said, only half-joking.

"You won't find it so funny when you're stuck in bed eating chicken soup for a month," Vanessa frowned, whipping away the jacket and holding it away from herself.

"And who's going to make that for me?"

Vanessa's mouth snapped shut at Emma's response. Emma turned her eyes away. There were some conversations that shouldn't be started.

It was too late.

"Have you…" Vanessa began, her attempt at caution palpable.

"Don't," Emma cut in, a barrier rising instantly.

"I worry, you know. That's all." The waitress held her hands up apologetically, although Emma could only see the gesture in her peripheral vision. "Emma…" she continued.

"Really. Don't."

The last thing she wanted was to start crying here, in public.

Instead, Emma let her eyes scan the menu, even though she knew already what she was going to order.

So did Vanessa.

"The usual?" she asked, not bothering to take the tatty notepad out of her pocket.

Emma gave a single nod, agreeing and putting a stop to the conversation in one movement.

Vanessa hovered as though deciding whether to persevere, but Emma was already pulling her phone from her pocket.

With a final shake of her head, Vanessa went to the counter, leaving Emma alone.

Emma clicked open her phone and stared at the screen. No missed calls. No new messages.

Letting out a deep sigh, she scrolled through her texts.

"I need to talk to you," she mumbled, beneath her breath.

Vanessa already thought she was losing it. Letting the waitress catch her talking to herself was the last thing Emma needed.

From where she was sitting, Emma could see straight through the café to the street out front, and the rain hammering against the floor to ceiling windows. It didn't look as though it was going to let up anytime soon.

If Angeline was with her, she would have insisted on taking one of the tables near the door. One of Angeline's favourite pastimes was people watching, making wild assumptions about the men and women walking past on the street outside. That man with the beanie hat is a bitcoin millionaire, but he doesn't want people to know. The woman over there with the pram? She's a nanny for a high-profile influencer. Vanessa is working undercover. She's not really a waitress, she's trying to expose a human trafficking ring right here in Maplewood.

Despite the dull throb of the migraine hangover and the tension she couldn't shake, Emma smiled to herself. She looked around the room, casting her eyes over the rag tag clientele. What would Angeline make of tonight's scattering of coffee lovers?

Before she had time to tap a message out to her sister, a white mug filled with steaming latte slid into view.

"Here you go," Vanessa said, looking at Emma's phone rather than her face. "Extra hot, just how you like it."

"Thanks," Emma said, slipping her phone back into her jacket and pulling the coffee towards her.

Rather than leaving to let Emma drink alone, Vanessa stood, hovering beside the table for a moment before speaking.

"What are you doing, Emma? Tonight. What are you doing?"

Emma sipped at the too hot latte, buying time, and shook her head.

"You're..." Vanessa started again.

"Yes. Okay. I'm obviously doing exactly what you think I'm doing. I'm here in your shitty little café, drinking alone. You've got me, alright?"

Vanessa shook her head. "Go home, Em. Don't do this. Angel wouldn't want..."

"You have no idea what Angeline would or wouldn't want. And please. Don't call her Angel. She hates it. She..." Emma cut herself short, biting her lip. "Just don't."

Vanessa looked over her shoulder into the main area of the café, confirming there weren't any other customers waiting for her attention, and took the seat opposite Emma. Her figure was of someone who helped themselves to too many of the end-of-day leftover cookies on a regular basis, so she pushed the chair away from the table to slide into place.

Despite Vanessa's move, Emma didn't protest. Even when Vanessa reached across and put her hands gently over the girl's, she remained silent.

"What do you think is going to happen?"

Emma said nothing.

"What are you trying to prove?"

This time Emma let her eyes rise to meet Vanessa's; nevertheless, she didn't speak.

"There's nothing you can do," Vanessa said, her voice as sweet as the caramel drizzle Emma only let herself have on special occasions. "You know that, don't you?"

Emma shook her head, almost imperceptibly.

"Look," Vanessa said. "I don't want to speak out of turn, you know. I wouldn't…I mean, I don't want to sound like I'm telling you what to do. I'm not your momma." She smiled, but the expression was laced with more than a hint of anxiety.

"So don't," Emma said. She kept her tone calm, but the effort of it showed.

"I have a bad feeling," Vanessa said, her voice a low whisper. "Why don't I box you up a slice of the apple cake you like? Maybe I can run to another coffee? You take them home, get out of the rain?"

Emma looked away, but the waitress could still see the tears pooling in her eyes.

"You know I can't do that," she said. "I…I can't do that."

"You can," Vanessa insisted. "You could. See, you wait here, I'll go…"

Emma inhaled, one long slow heavy breath.

There was no use in fighting. Not with Vanessa, anyway.

"Okay," she said. "Apple cake sounds…like an offer I can't refuse."

She forced a small, tight smile and hoped the older woman would believe her. There was no way she was going to head home, but what was the point in arguing? If she agreed to the cake and the coffee, Vanessa would leave her alone.

Vanessa paused, as though weighing up Emma's response to see if it was a full truth.

"Okay," Emma said again, nodding, trying to play out the bluff.

"You can't chase Angeline forever," Vanessa said as she stepped away.

"Yeah," Emma said in a near whisper. "I know."

But she could, and she knew that she would.

As Vanessa headed back to the counter, Emma took out her phone and placed it on the table next to her mug. She would drink half her latte first, before she called again.

She was used to making these deals with herself.

She was used to lying.

She picked up the phone and dialled.

Before the third ring sounded, the phone was ripped from Emma's hand.

"Stop it!" The words came from Vanessa, not Emma. "Please. Don't."

Emma stared at the waitress, phone in one hand and brown takeout bag in the other.

"This isn't helping anyone. Not you, and obviously not Angeline."

"What if it is?" Emma's voice cracked as she spoke.

Vanessa shook her head and thrust the contents of her hands towards Emma.

"Get out," she said, indicating the path to the door. "Just go."

Emma's eyes flicked automatically to her part-drunk latte.

"I don't care," Vanessa said, pre-empting the protestation. "Go."

Emma kicked back her chair and grabbed the bag and phone from the waitress's hands.

"Thanks," she said bitterly. "Thanks a lot."

As she walked away, grabbing her coat from the hook as she passed, Vanessa's voice came after her.

"This isn't what she would want, Emma."

It's not what I want either, Emma thought as she pushed open the door and stepped back out onto the pavement.

Emma sniffed, and freezing air shot into her nostrils.

Leaving the warmth of Urban Grind, Emma immediately felt the sharp contrast of the cold evening air. She slipped the package containing the apple cake into her bag and struggled into her jacket. Emma zipped it up quickly, trying to retain some of the cafe's warmth against the chill. However, the rain, falling steadily and coldly, seemed to target her the moment she stepped outside, relentlessly hitting her face. She pulled her hood up in an attempt to protect herself, but the raindrops found their way around, soaking her skin and chilling her to the bone.

The street was slick, reflecting the neon signs and streetlights in a kaleidoscope of colours on the pavement. Each step she took echoed in the evening's quiet, a solitary rhythm that matched the pounding in her chest.

Emma pulled her coat tighter around herself, the fabric still damp from earlier. The cold seeped through, biting at her skin, a stark contrast to the warmth of the café she had just left. The buzz of the heated argument with Vanessa still rang in her ears, mingling with the haunting silence of the high street. This part of town, once bustling and lively, now lay deserted as the evening drew on, its emptiness amplifying her solitude.

Emma's mind raced as she walked. The conversation with Vanessa had left her feeling exposed, raw. She was used to guarding her feelings, keeping her worries locked away where they couldn't hurt her—or anyone else. But Vanessa's words had sliced through her defences, reminding her of the reality she was trying to escape. Each step felt heavier, burdened with the weight of what she left behind in the café: a concerned friend, a half-drunk coffee, and a plea to stop chasing shadows.

The wind picked up, tugging at her coat and whipping her hair across her face. She stopped for a moment, closing her eyes against the gust. When she opened them again, she noticed a figure standing under the awning of a closed bookstore across the street. Startled, she stared at the silhouette, her eyes widening. The figure seemed to watch her, a stationary sentinel in the night. Paranoia tightened its grip around her throat. Was she being followed, or was her mind playing tricks on her? The isolation of the street, the eerie quiet, and the shadowy figure—all these elements swirled together, creating a tapestry of fear.

Her hand tightened on her phone.

Her lifeline.

Her ball and chain.

She had places to go, things to do. She didn't have time to follow shadows. Still, Emma considered crossing the street to confront the figure, to chase away those shadows with the light of reality, but hesitation held her back. Instead, she turned down a side street, hoping to loop back towards the main road further up. She knew every road in the entire town. Her whole life had been spent there, just as Angeline's had.

As she hastened her steps, the sound of her own breathing became ragged, mirroring the erratic beating of her heart. Emma knew she was letting fear get the better of her, but her run in with Vanessa and the isolation of her path conspired to fray the edges of her composure.

By the time she emerged back onto the main road, her body was tense, her mind teetering on the brink of panic. She cast a quick glance back towards the bookstore, but the figure was gone, leaving her to wonder if it had been nothing more than a figment of her imagination, a ghost conjured from her fears and the stress of the night.

Not just this night.

The stress of many nights.

The stress of every night that Angeline was not at home with her.

The realisation that she might be unravelling, that her grip on reality might be weaker than she feared, was perhaps the most terrifying thought of all. With a shuddering breath, Emma forced herself to focus on the pavement ahead, to put one foot in front of the other, to keep moving despite the fear, despite the despair. The weight of the night was heavy, but she would carry it, as she had carried so much already. Not because she wanted to, but because she had to.

She needed to follow Angeline.

No.

She needed to stop.

But she couldn't.

Not tonight.

Not ever.

SEVEN

Now

David cleared his throat and looked across at the girl, automatically slowing as he did. He felt a responsibility to make conversation, just as he did when Charlotte was his passenger.

She wanted to sit with her earphones plugged in, scrolling through whatever it was on her phone that she found far more interesting than her father. This was always the way. When Amanda travelled with them, when he wasn't running a taxi service to pick Lottie up from a block away from where she had been hanging out with her friends, Charlotte would chat away to her mother as though it was the most natural thing in the world. As if she didn't block him out whenever they were alone.

"That's what young adults are like," Amanda would tell him. "They don't want to hang around with Daddy."

She still wants to call me Daddy.

She still wants me around when she needs something.

No, that was harsh. Hadn't she been filled with sweetness and light earlier? Perhaps the slightest bit moody, but otherwise…

You're paying for her takeaway. She's got the house to herself.

No, that wasn't right. Amanda was at home. He had barely had time to think about what he was going to say to Amanda. He didn't have time to think about it now. When he had got rid of the girl, he could focus on the important issues.

She was at home, and that was for the best.

No more hanging out with her friend, Michael Johnson.

David coughed, bringing a hand up to cover his mouth. The steering wheel slipped, and the car jerked to the left.

"Sorry," he said.

The girl didn't even look up. She was engrossed in a purple block of pixels that was sliding down her phone screen.

"It…it could have happened a while ago," David said, and then wished he hadn't.

"Uh-huh," the girl replied.

"I mean…"

"I'd rather not think about it, if you don't mind," she said. The purple brick crashed down and the next fell awkwardly on top of it. "Frick. Thanks, David."

The girl clicked her phone closed and threw it onto her lap.

She sighed and looked over at him.

"I'm sorry," she said. "I've had a pretty crappy day, and this is all just…" She gestured in the air, mimicking the sudden burst of an explosion.

"Well, we have that in common," he said, not able to find a smile. "My day has been…less than great."

"Still," she said. "I'm lucky to be here, right?"

It was the second time she had used that word. *Lucky.* Her presence in the car certainly wasn't planned, so fate must have intervened in some way. Were fate and luck the same thing?

Not always.

Unless bad luck counts too.

"Lucky, you say?" David asked. "How so?"

"Sounds like there are some sickos out on these streets."

She had been demurely quiet since getting in the car, but something in her tone seemed to have changed. David shifted in his seat and looked back at the road.

"I thought you didn't…" David began. He stopped himself and instead asked, "Sickos?"

"Are you going to repeat everything I say?" the girl asked. Her voice had a playful tone that David tried to put down to nerves.

"No," he said. "I'm sorry. That woman. I'm sure…"

He wasn't sure of anything and didn't know where to take the sentence.

"What did you think of…what the reporter said?" the girl pressed on, undeterred.

"Uh," David stumbled.

"I think that a couple out walking their dog in the woods at this time only means one thing."

David's hands slipped on the wheel, causing the car to jolt to the left.

"Huh?"

"D-O-G-G-I-N-G," the girl spelt out. "You olds know about that, don't you?"

David almost laughed, but stopped the sound as it rose in him. She was twenty-one, and an adult, of course, but something about talking about such things seemed wrong.

He was a stranger in a car.

It was late.

She should be more careful.

Charlotte would never…

He shot the girl a look and replied.

"We *Olds* know about a lot of things. I'm more surprised…"

"That I do? What age is your kid again?"

David tightened his lips.

Charlotte was nothing like this girl.

Nothing at all.

He had to say something. His words tumbled out.

"Are you not slightly more concerned about the fact that a young woman has been murdered, not far from where I picked you up tonight? Not far from where you were wandering about in the dark, in the middle of nowhere…"

The girl let David's sentence trail off before responding, but when she did, she let fly.

"Well, firstly, Sherlock, I didn't hear them say that she had been murdered. As I recall, the shaky woman said that the circumstances were unclear. For all we know, she went out, got lost, got cold, ran into a bear or something."

David's outburst had apparently given the girl the green light to go off on one of her own. He cut her short.

"I know you're smart enough to know that there aren't any bears around here."

"But there's rain. It's freezing. I thought *I* was going to die back there. Before you kindly ordained to come back and give me a lift."

The silence between them was ice cold.

The girl cut through it.

"I didn't think you were going to stop."

"What gave you that idea? Was it when I saw you and kept driving?" David surprised himself with his response. He had sunk to her level of dark humour.

A woman was dead.

A woman had died within ten miles of where the two of them had met.

At least one of them should be afraid.

The girl shrugged.

"I'm here now, aren't I?" she said, her voice flat.

There was another brief silence between driver and passenger, before the girl spoke again.

"So, do you think they were dogging?" she laughed.

"Jeez," David said. "You're pretty dark."

He cast another glance at his passenger. She was fiddling with her phone again, its bright screen illuminating her face once more.

"Yeah," she said. "People say that about me. It's my style, you know. I try to own it these days. Listen, do you want to hear a joke?"

"Hmm?" He thought that he probably did not, but there wasn't a polite way to refuse.

"I've got a good one. It seems appropriate. You know…" She gestured between the two of them and then paused for a moment as though finding her words.

She began. "There's this guy hitchhiking…I mean, it could have been a girl, but let's go for guy. For the purposes of the joke."

"Did anyone ever tell you that you have great comic timing?" David asked. "If they did, they were lying."

"Okay, okay," the girl said. "There's this guy hitchhiking on a forest road. It's dark. Raining probably. He's been there for hours. No sign of a car. Nothing. Zilch. Then, finally, he hears the rumble of a distant engine. Lights pop up over the horizon behind him."

"Is it still a horizon if it's behind him?"

"Shush," the girl said, batting at David again. "Let me tell the joke."

"It's funny so far," he said.

He could never be like this with Charlotte. Nor with Amanda, for that matter. There was no room for frivolous comments with the women in his life. Everything he said was taken literally, a personal affront against one, the other, or usually both mother and daughter.

The girl was dark, but he was starting to lighten up to her.

She, on the other hand, seemed to be getting pissed with him.

"Oh, forget it," she sighed, and cut off her joke midway.

"I'm sorry," David said. He had lost count of the number of apologies he had given the girl, but it was still less than the amount he would have said to his wife and daughter by now.

"Whatever," the girl smiled, batting her hand. "It wasn't that funny anyway."

The girl pulled her knees up to her chest and put her feet up on the dashboard. She was settling in, getting comfortable. Too comfortable.

David saw her, and a prickle of anxiety made his breath catch in his throat.

"Don't sit like that," he said, more fatherlike than he had intended.

She shot him a look, which he caught in his peripheral vision.

"It's dangerous," he sighed. "I don't give a crap about the car. It's not mine, not really. It's just…it's not safe to sit like that. I'm always telling…well…"

"Your daughter?"

Now David turned his head to look at the girl.

"Yeah," he said. "But…" He paused for a moment, wondering whether to bother with the explanation, whether talking to her would make any difference. It hadn't so far with Lottie.

"But what?" the girl asked, almost playful, part goading him.

"Okay," he said, decision made. "See what it says on the dash there? Just beneath your feet." He gestured, and she leant forward to look. "If we were to get into an accident, even a minor one, the airbag system would deploy with incredible force. It's meant to protect you, but if your feet are up there," he paused again, waving towards the dashboard, "it could cause serious injury. The impact from the airbag could force your knees back towards your face or chest."

He let that sink in for a moment, watching her reaction as closely as he could while still focussing on the road, trying to gauge whether his message was getting through. Her feet were still on the dash, so he guessed not.

"Airbags blast out at 200 miles per hour in just a fraction of a second. Imagine that kind of force hitting your legs. It's not just about broken bones; it can lead to more severe, life-altering injuries," David continued, his tone earnest.

He hoped to strike a chord of awareness, not fear. He knew he sounded like a dad, but maybe that was the way she needed to hear it.

"I just want us both to be safe, you know?" David concluded, offering a small, reassuring smile.

"If my legs get blasted off," the girl said, "or whatever, I think *you* will probably still be safe."

David raised his hands from the steering wheel and thudded them down hard. His exasperation was too intense to conceal.

"Woah!" the girl said. "Okay, Daddy. Chill. I was messing with you, alright?"

She pulled her knees back in towards herself and lowered her feet to the floor.

"I'm sorry…" he began. "I mean, I don't even know you. I just…"

"You have a kid around my age. Sure. I get it."

David shrugged a short apology.

He looked across at her again.

She was so similar to Lottie, and yet so different.

Charlotte would never leave the house so late at night.

Charlotte rarely left the house at all.

The thought jarred in David's head. Was it really such a positive thing that his daughter spent so much time in her room, alone, instead of venturing out into the world?

A woman was dead.

A girl was in his car.

Should he…

His thoughts were decimated by the girl's screamed words.

"Watch out!"

EIGHT

David Three Hours Ago

The venue that Mitchell, or whoever organised that kind of thing for him, had chosen for the awards ceremony was Henderson House. Once a stately manor, now it was merely a venue for training, team building, and nights such as this. David pulled into the driveway and made his way up towards the house.

His nervousness showed no sign of relenting; his heart jittered in his chest like an agitated bird. Drawing up to the venue only made the fluttering more intense.

He wasn't ready. He hadn't spent enough time preparing. He was distracted by Amanda's absence. More than that, he couldn't stop thinking about what Charlotte had said to him.

There was no time for any of those excuses. Stopping in the vast car park, he let the engine continue its purr as he stared into the rearview mirror. He had arrived early, as he always did. The LED clock read 20:05, but the area was already starting to fill for the eight thirty start.

His car, a mid-size sedan, blended in with the line of similar dark-coloured Accords. All part of the same fleet. All part of the company's uniform blandness.

Wasn't that what he liked about Tursten Mitchell, though? Everyone was treated the same. He was grateful, in part, that each of them had a company car. It was one less area for competition. Even Malcolm Mitchell, the CEO, drove the same grey Honda, although David knew from experience that the boss's car had a bespoke interior. Where his own cream leather seats seemed luxurious, Mitchell's were butter soft. The dash in Malcolm's car was a polished walnut that made David's standard edition seem almost drab by comparison.

Now, though, sitting in his own driver's seat, thinking about the night ahead, none of that mattered.

What mattered tonight was the award.

What mattered tonight was finally being recognised.

David looked up at the mirror, checked over his appearance, and tried to smile.

"Thank you," he said, but the words sounded dull and artificial.

It was already getting dark outside. The gravel car park was lined with pristine silver birch trees, and his headlights bounced off the white bark, making them look like the doric columns on the building that was to host the ceremony. That was up ahead, a short walk further along the drive, away from where the attendees had been told to park.

If he sat in the car a while longer, the rain might let up. He didn't want to dig in the trunk for his umbrella when there was the possibility that he could get away without it.

He would wait, and while he did, he would practise the damn speech.

"Thank you –"

A sharp triple tap on the side window brought David back into the moment with a jolt.

He could see the man's mouth moving, but couldn't hear anything through the thick glass.

It was Johnson.

Six foot five of smarmy arsehole leaned against the side of David's car, head bent to look inside. Michael Johnson.

Johnson had an umbrella, of course. Clenched in his left hand like a weapon. An image flashed through David's mind of exactly what he would like to do with that umbrella, but he pushed it away, and did what he always did.

He forced a smile.

Reluctantly, David pressed the button to lower the window.

"Hey. You coming in or are you planning on spending the night in the car park?" Michael peered further into the car. "Not having a crafty fag in here, are you? You know that's not allowed, Burny." As if an afterthought had struck him, Michael glanced into the back seat.

David clenched his teeth at the sound of the bastardisation of his name that Michael insisted on using. How would *he* like it if he started referring to him as Johnny? It was too petty; he couldn't go there.

"Michael, good evening," David said, cordially, instead.

"No Mandy tonight?" Michael asked, with a boyish lightness to his tone. "Better things to do?"

His question was somewhere between curious and sarcastic.

"Er, no," David said, cursing internally that he hadn't thought up an excuse. He had been so hung up on the speech and too irritated by Amanda's decision not to join him. He'd skipped the details, and now Michael was going to make him pay for it.

"That's a shame. It's always a pleasure to see the beauty with the beast."

"What can I say?" David said. He was beginning to feel uncomfortable, sitting behind the wheel with Johnson looming over the car. He cleared his throat and spoke again.

"I was waiting for the rain to stop," he said. "I see you're prepared, as always."

His colleague liked that; David could tell.

"Oh yes," he said. "Della insisted on her own, of course. Wifey doesn't like to get too close to me in public. Cramps her style, you know." He hollered out a hearty exaggerated laugh before adding, "You can come under with me if you like?"

David thought for a moment about the black fold up he had in the trunk and wished he had brought it out sooner. Why hadn't he just got out of the car as soon as he parked up? Why did there always have to be another minute of looking in the mirror?

With a sigh, David said, "That's very kind, mate. Thank you."

He'd read somewhere about the Benjamin Franklin effect – if you ask someone to do you a favour, they are more likely to like you. Even though he wasn't the one, this time, to ask for assistance, he never turned down the offer of help from his coworker. It was in part to do with the theory and in part that he wanted to do anything he could to inconvenience Michael.

They had the same job role, sat in the same corner of the office, went after the same projects. They could never have hoped to become friends.

David switched off the engine and pushed open the door, stepping under Michael's waiting umbrella.

"Really," he said. "Thanks."

"Don't worry about it," Michael said. "What's mine is yours. What's yours is mine, right?" He coughed out a low, throaty laugh and stood back so David could walk with him, shielded from the rain.

"Della," Michael said with a snap of his fingers. "Come."

It sounded for all the world that he was calling to a pet dog rather than his pretty blonde wife.

And she *was* attractive. David's eyes lingered over her a little too long as he followed Michael's voice across the car park. Slim in a way that showed she had never had children, pale skin that made her fair hair look natural, whether or not it truly was.

"Alright, Burny. Not everything that's mine is yours, eh?" Michael quickened his pace, meaning that David had to speed up too to stay beneath the umbrella.

His feet crunched across the gravel, and he looked down to check that his polished black leather shoes weren't in danger of stepping into puddles. It wasn't so much them he was worried about, but kicking mud up his rented tux would not be a good look when he got up on the stage.

It was a longer walk to the house than David had expected. The journey was punctuated by Michael swinging the umbrella over his own head, leaving David in the rain on multiple occasions.

He doesn't mean to.

David's thought was more to stop himself from becoming annoyed than to rationalise the other man's behaviour.

The trio's slow progression toward the grand house felt interminable under the heavy sky, weighed down further by the undercurrents of tension between David and Michael. Each step seemed to echo with unspoken rivalries, the crunch of gravel underfoot punctuating the silence that stretched between exchanges.

"Del, come on," Michael called over his shoulder. The woman was teetering behind in heels that looked too dangerous to walk in on the uneven terrain.

If Amanda were there, she would insist on holding on to David's arm. He would put up a display of feigned irritation, as he always did, but underneath, the warmth of being useful to her would glow.

He was a gentleman.

He was a damn good guy.

He deserved tonight.

As they approached the illuminated entrance, the grandeur of the venue became apparent, its lights casting long shadows that danced across the path. David couldn't help but admire the stately architecture, so different from the mundane office building where he spent his days. Yet, the beauty of the moment was overshadowed by Michael's incessant chatter, primarily directed at Della, but with the occasional jibe thrown David's way, thinly veiled as camaraderie.

"Looking forward to the awards, Burny?" Michael's voice cut through the night, a hint of mockery lacing his words. "I've heard the competition's stiff this year."

David offered a non-committal grunt, unwilling to engage. His thoughts were preoccupied with the night's significance. Michael's presence, with his effortless charm and casual arrogance, served as a constant reminder of the competition between them, not just for awards but for professional standing and respect within the company.

Della, seemingly oblivious to the tension, adjusted her grip on her clutch and smiled at David.

"It's going to be a wonderful evening, don't you think? Malcolm has outdone himself with the venue this year."

"Yes, it looks incredible," David managed, forcing a smile in return.

His gaze briefly met Della's, and he was struck by the genuine warmth in her expression, a stark contrast to Michael's smirking demeanour. It made him wonder what she saw in Michael, or what unseen facets Michael kept hidden from the workplace. He couldn't be that much of a douche if he could pull a woman like this, and keep hold of her after – how long had they been together?

As they finally reached the entrance, the trio was greeted by the soft hum of conversations and the gentle clinking of glasses from within. The atmosphere was charged with anticipation, the air thick with the scent of expensive perfume and the underlying fragrance of ambition.

David felt Michael's hand clasp his shoulder, pressing damp cloth against his skin. It was a gesture that might have seemed friendly to onlookers but felt loaded with condescension to David. "Let's make our entrance, shall we? After all, we're the men of the hour."

Pulling away slightly, David nodded, his expression neutral. "After you," he said, gesturing for Michael to lead the way.

As Michael strode forward, David took a moment to steady himself, drawing in a deep breath. Tonight was about more than just awards; it was a test of his resolve, a challenge to stand tall amidst the shadows of doubt and rivalry.

Stepping into the venue, David couldn't shake the feeling of being on the brink of something significant. The night was laden with possibilities, each more daunting than the last. As he followed Michael and Della into the heart of the gathering, the weight of the unspoken battles between them hung heavy in the air, a silent storm brewing on the horizon of the night's festivities.

With every step, though, he felt his wife's absence. All his colleagues were accompanied by their partners. He stood out as being the only one to have come alone.

She should have been here was matched only by *I should have thought of a decent explanation* in David's mind.

"Quite the turnout, isn't it?" Michael remarked, his voice echoing slightly in the vastness of the foyer. The murmur of gathered colleagues and competitors filled the space, a blend of anticipation and courteous rivalry. David nodded, his eyes scanning the crowd, noting the mix of eager and envious faces.

Their arrival didn't go unnoticed. A few heads turned, conversations momentarily pausing as they took in the trio. David felt a twinge of satisfaction at the attention, fleeting though it was.

He could put up with Michael Johnson's company.

He could forgive Amanda for not being with him.

He was finally going to have something to be remembered for.

Everything was about to change.

NINE

Emma Three Hours Ago

Emma had been thrown out of bars before – mostly because of Angeline's behaviour rather than her own – but she had never been ejected from a coffee shop. There was a particular irony to it.

If she had ever had any 'bad girl' days, they were behind her. Gone were the wild, carefree nights out. She and Angeline painting the town whatever damn colours they liked. Gone, gone, gone.

Her footsteps quickened on the wet pavement, the sound echoing in the evening's quiet. Despite wanting to dig her hands deep into her pockets and keep them in there, warm, protected against the weather, her urge to use her phone was too great. She pulled it out, sleeves pulled down as far as possible over her hands, and tapped on the screen.

She wouldn't mention her detour.

No need for anyone else to know she was losing her mind.

"I've left the coffee place," she said. "I say left, but well, don't be mad, but they asked me to leave. Nessy…well…we had a *disagreement* of sorts."

"Anyway, it wasn't so bad. Nessy still gave me some apple cake and a freebie latte. I guess she was thinking of you. If it survives the journey, maybe we can have the cake together."

Emma moved the phone away from her face and pulled back her wrist to cover her mouth. A wave of nausea washed over her, and she fought to keep it at bay.

"Sorry," she said, eventually, when the feeling subsided. "Too much coffee. Too many meds. My head again. You know…"

Shaking her head, she hung up.

She kept walking. Her itinerary was fixed in her mind. Her path was plotted. Nothing was going to keep her from her destination. There were just a few stops to make along the way.

Emma came to a crossing, paused briefly at the curb, the blinking pedestrian light casting an intermittent glow on her face. She glanced left, then right, the street deserted except for the occasional passing car, their headlights cutting through the rain like searchlights in a storm. The town felt different at night, especially under the veil of rain—more solitary, more reflective, like it echoed her own internal turmoil.

Emma reached the other side of the street, her shoes splashing in puddles. Droplets bounced off the tarmac, creating miniature fountains. Despite the cold misery, there was still some beauty in the world.

As she approached the park, the rain seemed to let up, as if the universe itself was granting her a momentary reprieve. The iron gates loomed ahead, the entrance to what had once been their sanctuary, their escape from the world's prying eyes and harsh realities. Emma's heart beat a little faster, anticipation and dread mingling in her chest.

She slipped through the gates, her footsteps now silent on the wet grass. The park was shrouded in darkness, save for the occasional streetlamp that fought against the night.

"I wish you were here," she whispered into the night, her voice barely audible above the sound of the droplets falling from the leaves. "I really need you right now."

Emma had always thought that the park wasn't really a *park* in the true sense of the word.; it was more a couple of blocks in the middle of the town where they hadn't built apartments yet. It felt like a placeholder, a temporary green space amidst the urban sprawl. Still, it was called Pierce Park. There was a designated path, landscaped gardens and even a small duck pond, so to all intents, it was a park.

Past the flower beds that were trying their best to bloom, Emma winced as she looked at the largest of the grassed areas. A wide oblong area lay brown and twisted, flattened by the ice rink that the town hosted in the park each winter. As soon as Christmas had passed, the guys in the hi-vis vests came and dismantled the wonderland, leaving the grass below shrivelled, clinging on to life.

And it would spring up green again, as it did every year.

Now though, all it did was remind Emma of holding on to the side wall while Angeline span around the slick ice like a professional. It didn't matter. It was about the two of them spending time together. They were never in competition. Not with each other.

Afterwards, sitting on a bench with steaming cups of hot chocolate in their hands, Emma and Angeline watched the dwindling number of skaters on the ice rink, a vestige of the holiday cheer that had enveloped the park. With Christmas just a whisper away, the park was a tableau of festive joy, but Emma couldn't shake off a nagging feeling.

"It feels so artificial," Emma had finally said, breaking the comfortable silence between them. The twinkling lights from the rink cast a soft glow on her face, revealing a contemplative frown.

Angeline turned to her.

"But isn't it the buildings around us that are artificial? This park, this ice rink—they bring a bit of magic to the city. It's not the park's fault that the world outside is all concrete and steel."

Emma chuckled, a sound more melancholic than merry. "I'm not blaming the park," she admitted, her gaze wandering over the rink, watching as a child stumbled and was promptly lifted back to their feet by a laughing parent. "I guess I just wonder why we need to create these escapes rather than fix what makes us want to escape in the first place."

Angeline studied her sister for a long moment before responding, her voice soft but firm. "Why does anyone or anything need to be to blame? Can't we just appreciate a good thing in a freaking world of bad?"

Her face was so serious that Emma couldn't do anything but laugh. It was so easy, then.

"You're such an idiot," Emma said, pushing against the padding of Angelina's layers hard enough to flail to stay on the bench.

As Angeline opened her mouth to protest, waving her hands in a counter-attack, she was silenced by a piercing sound.

The two girls paused, mid-parry, and stared at each other, eyes wide.

"What was that?" Emma whispered, pulling Angeline back onto the bench, back beside her.

Angeline shuffled in closer, pressing herself against her sister. She shook her head.

"You think we should…? Where did it…?" Emma's hand grabbed Angeline's as she stretched her neck, lifting her head to locate the source of the noise.

It was a scream. A single sharp yelp of a scream. Unmistakable.

It was a woman.

And now, it had stopped.

Angeline buried her head into Emma's jacket.

"I don't like it," she murmured. "We should go."

Emma smoothed her sister's hair and kissed the top of her head.

"It's stopped now," she said. "Probably nothing."

Angeline nodded. "Kids," she said. "Messing about."

As she spoke, a hooded figure ran past them, clutching something in his arms. Then, from somewhere not far enough away from them to be ignorable, a woman's voice.

"Help! Someone!"

Angeline sunk her head back into the crook of Emma's arm.

"It's okay," Emma said. "Listen, let me have a look. You sit…"

Angeline cut in. "No, no, no. Please. It's not safe. It might not be safe. We shouldn't…"

"Someone might need us," Emma said, lifting Angeline away from her with tender care, and rising to her feet. "I'll just look, okay. We can phone the police if anything has happened. We don't need to get involved. Okay."

The look on Angeline's face was one of unconvinced concern, but she attempted a resigned nod.

The two girls moved cautiously, clinging on to each other as they walked towards the source of the scream.

Angeline's grasp was firm, and Emma placed her hand on top of her sister's.

As they rounded the corner, they saw the figure of a woman on the concrete path beneath the bridge.

A man was leaning over her, and as they looked on, he crouched down by the woman's side.

"Should we...?"

Angeline squeezed Emma's arm, stopping her in her tracks.

"I think he's got it," she whispered.

"But...I have to. We..."

Emma's expression sealed the deal. Angeline nodded, despite her reluctance, and pulled on towards the scene.

"Hey," Emma shouted, when they were within earshot.

The man looked up.

"Do you need anything?" Emma asked.

The man waved his phone. "I've called the emergency services."

Emma turned her attention to the woman, who was half-sitting now. Without a word, the woman smiled, and waved an arm.

Angeline shrugged.

"It's all in hand, I think," she said, not trying to mask the relief in her voice.

Emma nodded.

"Let's get out of here," Angeline said. "Shit, we need to be more careful."

"We've got each other," Emma said, gripping Angeline's arm firmly. "It's the world that needs to be more careful of us."

"That doesn't even make sense," Angeline laughed. "But I love you."

Emma looked over her shoulder as the sisters walked away, back past the ice rink, back to their warm, safe lives.

They never heard what happened to the woman, but still Emma thought of her. Two days after seeing her in the park, Angeline presented Emma with a gift. Now, with only herself to rely on, no Angeline by her side, Emma reached into her pocket and her hand met its cold shell. A blade, metal inside wood. Maybe tonight would be the time for her to use it.

The knife was a paradox of beauty and danger. Its smooth handle was inlaid with varnished walnut, and the sharp steel tucked neatly inside. The casual observer may not have even taken it for a weapon at all. It was a trinket. A symbol of Angeline's love and concern. Emma had always considered it a token of protection, never truly believing she'd have cause to use it.

She had it because Angeline had wanted her to have it. She carried it now because it reminded her of her sister. It was with her, and Angeline was not.

Emma wanted to reach for her phone, make another call that wouldn't be answered, speak words that would never be heard. Instead, she spoke into the night, her words coming out in foggy clouds.

"I wish you were here," she breathed again, as she kept on walking through the rain, into the darkness.

TEN

Now

David slammed his foot hard on the brake pedal. There was no time, now, to think about pumping slowly, being cautious. There was no time for rational thought. He slammed on the brake and the tyres screeched in protest.

Too late. It was too late.

His reactions were too slow.

Perhaps if he had jerked the wheel, tried to avoid it instead of attempting to stop.

Perhaps then.

But David had reacted, and the car thudded into the deer that the girl had seen, and he had not.

A shuddering *thuck* rippled through the car as it slammed into the creature.

This wasn't a fragile yearling, no echo of the shape by the roadside earlier, the shape that had turned out to be the girl.

This was a solid stag.

David's mind flashed back to when he had first spotted the girl by the side of the road. What if he hadn't been concentrating then? What if he had hit her?

Everything could change in the blink of an eye.

He had been careless, tonight.

The corner, too fast.

The stag, unseen.

The girl, in his car.

There were too many mistakes.

The car skidded as it came to a standstill. The stag stumbled, but stood, looking at the occupants with something that almost seemed like indignation, before turning tail and darting off into the woods.

"Shit!" the girl yelped.

"It's okay," David tried to calm her, despite not feeling at all calm himself. "It's okay. We are fine."

The car was still, now, stationary in the middle of the road. The engine hummed. The headlights shone on the road ahead. The stag was gone.

David swallowed hard, his hand reaching down beside him and again not finding his coffee cup.

He needed his fix. He could feel the tremor in his hands, the fluttering of his heart.

"We are fine, are we?" the girl asked. "Is this a regular evening for you?" Her voice was an adrenaline-fuelled, high-pitched squeak.

Maybe she needed a drink, too. Damn, they could probably both use something stronger than the vile instant machine brew he was forcing himself to look forward to. How much further was it to the truck stop? And was the car going to make it that far?

He could hardly call up the company funded roadside assistance service, even if he had a phone with any kind of cellular signal.

David almost laughed at the thought, but held himself back.

"Regular?" he said instead. "Sure. I do this all the time."

The girl shook her head and kicked open the passenger door.

"Where are you going?" David twisted his head down to look out of the side door to where she was standing in the road. "Twenty-One? Get back in. It was an accident."

She bent to look back at him.

"I know," she said. "But it was an *accident*. You need to check your car."

But I want to keep moving.

I need to keep moving.

David kept his thoughts to himself and nodded.

"Stay there then," he said. "I'll be right back."

The last thing he needed was for the girl to wander off, get lost, or worse.

Or perhaps that's what he *did* need. Picking her up had led to nothing but trouble, but he had found enough of that before he'd ever met the girl.

David stepped out into the night, his movements hesitant, as if getting out of the car made him more vulnerable. There was no sign of the storm quitting, but there was no need, now, to worry about getting his suit wet or messing up his styled hair. The night had gone far beyond that.

The chill of the forest air was a sharp contrast to the warmth that had cocooned him inside the vehicle, a reminder of the stark divide between the safe haven he had created and the unpredictability of the world beyond. In the car, he had been moving forwards. It felt like an escape, even though he was carrying his troubles with him.

The wet tarmac road squelched beneath David's shoes; the sound was unnervingly loud in the quiet that surrounded him. The headlights, still glaring into the darkness, illuminated the scene with an almost accusatory brightness, casting long, ominous shadows that stretched out on the road ahead. David approached the car's damaged front end with a reluctance that felt almost physical. If there was any serious damage, anything beyond superficial scrapes and scratches, they were going to need help, and there was no way he was going to get any.

He could almost see himself walking the rest of the way to the truck stop, hoping that a car would come past and give *him* a lift. He could become a passenger, put himself into the hands of someone else, let them take the wheel. It wasn't a terrible thought. Hadn't he always been the one in control, pushing forwards, taking everyone along with him? Had it got him anywhere? No. Never.

Even in the tension of the moment, walking towards the front of the car to assess the damage, the thought of ceding control was calming.

He flicked his gaze to the girl. She was leaning casually against the open passenger door, waving her phone in the air, arm extended. Trying and failing, to catch a signal.

I should let the girl drive. See where we end up.

The girl looked so innocent, so carefree: the opposite of his fractured, fragile existence. He had a wife and daughter who barely needed him, let alone loved him. He had a boss that didn't value or respect him. He had a trunk full of trouble, and he was just driving along with it, taking it with him on his so-called escape.

The girl seemed to feel his eyes on her, and she turned her head to return the stare.

With her free hand, she gave a shooing motion. Go. Get on with it.

David nodded at her wordless gesture and carried on to the front of the car.

The bumper bore the evidence of the encounter— a dent that was somehow both less and more severe than he had anticipated. A smattering of fur, caught in the grille, served as a tangible reminder of the deer, of the sudden, jarring intrusion of the wild into the manufactured calm of his journey. His fingers hovered over the indentation.

As he stood there, bathed in the artificial light of the headlights, David was acutely aware of the isolation of the road, of the enveloping darkness that seemed to press in from all sides. The night was vast, and he was but a single, solitary figure within it, momentarily cast adrift by the unforeseen. The silence of the surroundings weighed heavily upon him, a suffocating blanket that muffled the sound of his own breathing, rendering it eerily loud in his ears.

That was until the girl spoke.

"Do you always drive like that?"

The girl had moved around to the front of the car, and was leaning against the side of the bonnet, eyeing him as he ran his hand over the bumper.

He shot her a sharp look.

"I'm sorry," he said. "I…"

He didn't need supervision. He had everything under control.

"Why don't you wait in the car?" he suggested.

"Boring," she said, extending the vowels in the word.

Her coat was doing nothing to protect her from the elements.

"Aren't you cold?" he said, trying a different tack. There was no reason for her to examine the car. There was nothing for her to see.

The girl shook her head and pushed off, walking two paces closer to stand beside David.

"You trying to get rid of me?" she asked. "I'm afraid we're a team now. Me and you, on this road forever."

The look he gave her was raw: an unequivocal expression of horror. He turned his head away, aware of how he must look to her.

"I'm messing with you," she said. Her voice was calm. She seemed unshaken by his reaction, unshaken by the collision, unshaken by the night.

How did someone so young manage to stay so cool under pressure?

Lottie would be screaming at him by now. Then again, she would probably have got out of the car too and refused to get back in with such a dangerous, careless driver. Or was that her mother he was thinking of? Sometimes they were interchangeable in his mind.

Lottie would never be here in the first place.

Lottie was safe at home.

David let himself look back up at the girl.

Twenty-one. Was Charlotte going to change this much in two years? He shook his head and stood up. The light from the car's beams shone upon him, and he stepped back, away from the glare.

He didn't want to be examined. He didn't want to be seen. He wanted to sit, facing forwards in the security of the car's interior.

Still, the girl looked at him from beneath her eyelashes.

"You did almost kill me, though," she said.

The hint of a smile in her voice was almost reassuring. He didn't think he could handle a woman having a meltdown. He was grateful for her attitude.

"I have to say," David sighed. "You've certainly found your voice."

The girl stepped away from the car, her figure emerging into the wash of the headlights, casting her own elongated shadow across the tarmac.

"Doesn't look too bad," she nodded. "Did you see what happened to the…"

"Ran off," David said. "Headed into the trees, over there. Lucky he was such a big bastard."

The girl shrugged. "Guess so. Must have still hurt the poor guy, though. Being hit like that. How fast were you going?"

The tension was fading as they spoke.

The relief of the superficial damage to the car helped, but the girl's demeanour was even more calming.

David smiled, patted the dent and stepped back, too.

"I don't know. Slower than usual," he said, thinking back to his earlier skid out. "Look, there's no real damage. Let's get out of the rain."

With that, he walked around to the driver's door, but the girl stood stock still, watching him.

"Unless you want to wait for someone else to pick you up?" he called over the roof of the car.

"You almost killed me," the girl repeated in a sing-song tone.

Her hood was up, but the fabric was soaked through. It would not protect her for long.

"I'm sorry," David said again. "I'll get you a coffee at the rest stop to make up for it, okay?"

"I don't know if I should trust you," she said, tilting her head.

The girl looked around, almost furtively. Trees, road, trees. That's all there was. That and the car, and the two of them.

As David hovered by the open door, the silence between them thickened once more.

But it didn't last long.

David was about to remind the girl that they hadn't seen another car on the road, and assure her that being his passenger was safer than being out here on her own, taking her chances. He was about to until he heard the unmistakable hum of an engine.

They were no longer alone.

He froze, looking up the road, his vision blurred by the watery veil of the rain.

Lights. Not just the lemonade glow of headlights. A red and blue flicker was coming towards them.

The girl's attention also switched to the open road. She wiped at her face with her sleeve, drying it, sweeping droplets from her eyes, trying to focus, to see what David had seen.

"I don't think that's your lift," David said quietly as the car came closer.

He slipped into his familiar driver's seat and restarted the engine.

"Let's go, Twenty-One," he said,

As she looked into the distance, the look of confusion on the girl's face turned to recognition as she saw the oncoming vehicle, and then to something else – something David couldn't quite interpret.

"Twenty-One," he called again, trying not to let his anxiety show, "Let's go."

ELEVEN

David Two Hours Ago

Almost as soon as they had arrived, Michael broke away from David. Without so much as a word, he took Della by the arm and led her off into the throng.

No matter. David would have to spend enough time with them later. It wasn't worth feigning insincere offence at being left alone. He and Michael worked too closely together and had to compete too often for the juiciest contracts to be anything like friends. Outside of the office, if they had met socially rather than as coworkers, David doubted that the two of them would have had any cause to speak to each other at all.

Ever since he had met Amanda, though, his social circle had shrunk. There were a handful of old university chums that kept in touch for the major life events, but other than that, his life was Amanda and Charlotte. They were his world, and it was a world he loved, even if he sometimes felt like he was on the outside of it looking in.

I'm not antisocial, I'm asocial.

It wasn't that he wanted to avoid being with other people, he just didn't want to put in any kind of unnecessary effort to seek out friendship.

He was comfortable living life as a lone wolf.

He already had everything he needed.

The problem tonight was that what he needed – who he needed – was at home, and he was here. With Amanda beside him, he could have relaxed into the night. They would have stood on the sidelines, shared private jokes, soaked in the atmosphere. Alone, he knew there was something missing.

Amanda, Amanda, Amanda.

David moved through the crowd like a ghost, his presence barely registering to the clusters of colleagues who congregated around tables laden with champagne flutes and hors d'oeuvres. He plucked one of the long-stemmed glasses as he passed, heading towards the Grand Hall. He didn't intend on drinking, but he felt naked enough there alone, at least if he was holding a drink, he had something in common with the hundreds of other Tursten Mitchell employees and guests.

He fitted in, in his rented black tux and ridiculous bow tie. All the men were dressed similarly, apart from the odd outliers who thought that a dinner jacket was adequate for such a formal event. The wives were more of a mish-mash of styles. Some had picked out short cocktail dresses, others wore long flowing silks. What had Amanda bought for the occasion? He couldn't remember if she had shown him her dress. It would have been new, and it would definitely not have been a hire outfit.

Had she ever meant to be with him tonight?

If Amanda had given notice she was going to let him down – because that's what she was doing, wasn't it? – he might have made a backup plan.

'Always have a backup plan,' he thought.

Life was full of teachable moments, and that was the biggie that he was taking away from tonight.

He should have seen the signs. The absence of a dress was one. Had she had her hair done today? He should have paid more attention. He should always pay her more attention. That was one teachable moment he didn't need.

Now, David leant against the wall, alone, holding a glass of champagne that he would never drink. Rather than butterflies in his stomach, the churning dread was so severe it felt like wasps. He checked his watch and wished there was less time to fill before the start of the award-giving. He didn't know how long he could bear this.

Across the room, he could see Michael and Della. They shone under an invisible spotlight, their laughter ringing out, drawing others into their orbit. Della, with her hair cascading in waves of gold, leaned into Michael, her hand resting lightly on his arm. Michael, ever the raconteur, was in his element. His stories, which David mercifully could not hear, were punctuated by bursts of laughter from those who hung on his every word.

He could see his mouth moving, the effluent gestures his colleague made; he was glad it was someone else's turn to listen.

Still, David took a step towards them, then hesitated. A part of him yearned to be within that circle of light, to feel the warmth of belonging. Yet, another part, the part that nursed a growing ember of resentment, kept him rooted to the spot, a spectator rather than a participant.

As if sensing his gaze, Michael turned, locking eyes with David across the room. A knowing smile crept across Michael's face, one that seemed to say, '*I see you there, lurking.*'.

Michael excused himself from the group and made his way over, Della in tow, her elegance casting shadows on David's already dimming spirit.

"David, my man! Not hiding, are you? You look like a bit of a sore thumb, stuck out here on your own." Michael's voice was jovial, but his eyes held a glint of something David couldn't quite place. Amusement? Pity? Contempt?

"Just taking it all in," David replied, forcing a smile that felt more like a grimace. He moved his head closer to Michael. "It's loud in here, eh?"

Michael clapped him on the shoulder, a gesture that felt too familiar, too intimate. "You know, Amanda mentioned something about enjoying her quiet nights in. Says there's nothing like a good book and a glass of wine to make her forget about the dull roar of these events."

The mention of Amanda's name, casual as it might have been, struck David like a physical blow. He stiffened, the smile freezing on his lips.

"Did she now?" he said. His voice was steady, but he could feel the storm brewing behind his calm facade.

"Oh, yes. Mandy and I chat about all sorts of things. You know how it is," Michael continued, oblivious or indifferent to the effect his words might have.

Not once had David ever referred to his wife as *Mandy*, and he didn't want to think of the response he would get if he tried. She was too elegant for such a contraction.

"She prefers *Amanda*," David said, with more ice in his voice than he had planned.

"Not *Mrs Burnham*?" Michael smiled. "Well, she's never told me off so far." He actually nudged David in the ribs, like a schoolboy trying to highlight the fact that he had got one over on his buddy.

They were not buddies, though. They never would be.

Della, picking up on the undercurrents, tipped her empty champagne flute at Michael and stepped away wordlessly to refresh her drink, leaving the two men in an uneasy standoff.

David searched Michael's face for signs of deceit, for the hint of a lie. But all he found was the calm confidence of a man who believed he held the upper hand.

"I wasn't aware you two were so close," David managed, each word laced with a venom he could barely contain.

"Ah, well, we all have our secrets, don't we, David?" Michael's smile widened, but his eyes were cold. "Anyway, best of luck tonight. Though, between you and me, I think we both know who the real winner is."

David stood open-mouthed, wishing he could think of a snappy comeback. Later, long after it mattered, something would come to him as it always did.

I should have said that, he would think, but it would be too late.

"Anyway," Michael smiled, his eyes wandering across the room. "I'd better go and keep up with my lovely wife. Can't leave them alone for a minute, can you?"

"Apparently not," David said, gritting his teeth.

"See you for the main event, mate." Michael's smile broke into a wide grin, before he turned to rejoin the festivities.

As Michael walked into the crowd, leaving David in the wake of his insinuations, a torrent of emotions threatened to overwhelm him. Jealousy, anger, betrayal—all swirling into a toxic brew that threatened to spill over.

David was left standing alone, the noise of the party fading to background static. His thoughts raced, a maelstrom of doubts and fears converging on a single, inescapable conclusion: something was terribly, irrevocably wrong. And when something was wrong in his life, it came down to one of two things: Amanda or Michael. This time, perhaps, it was both.

David's grip on the champagne glass's thin stem tightened, like a hand around a slim throat. He wasn't going to drink it; he never touched a drop, especially when he was driving.

His entire body pounded with the tense impulse to get out of there and go home. He wanted to talk to his wife. He wanted to see his daughter. Most of all, he didn't want to spend another second in the same building as Michael Johnson.

If it wasn't for the award, if it wasn't for the fact that it was the most important night of his life, he would have let the impulse take over. He would have left. He could have left. But the night meant everything.

David was lost in his own thoughts when, unexpectedly, he heard someone address him.

"Quite the turnout, eh?" the voice said into David's ear.

He turned slightly, surprised at being spoken to, and came face to face with Malcolm Mitchell.

"Sir," David said, his instincts taking over. "Wonderful venue, sir."

Mitchell nodded, tilting his champagne glass.

"I hope you're prepared for this, Burnham," Michell said, reaching out a hand and patting David's arm. "Things are going to change back at the office after tonight."

The adrenaline rush surging through David's vein seemed to stop in its tracks at the CEO's words.

"Sir?" David half-asked. He needed to work on his responses. First Michael, now he couldn't find a suitable reply for the most important man in the room.

Always be ready to impress.

But he wasn't impressing anyone; he was floundering.

Malcolm Mitchell's face was serious, studying David's reaction for a moment, before he looked past him, over towards the makeshift stage that had been set up for the occasion.

"Better snap to it and find your table, lad. Looks like I'm being summoned."

David turned his head to see that Mitchell's PA was waving at the CEO from across the room.

"Sir," David repeated and wished he hadn't. He tilted his champagne glass towards his boss's to clink them together, but before they touched,

Mitchell had already started to stride towards the stage.

Be calm.

There's nothing to worry about.

This is my night.

Things are going to change.

Repeating the words in his head, he headed for the seating plan that was set on an A-frame easel. He scanned the board to find his table. Number one. Of course. Next to Johnson. Of course.

All the better to stick it to him.

David managed to smile at the thought. He could get through anything for the satisfaction of bringing the award back to the table, making Johnson look at it while their coworkers flapped around him, cooing over his achievement.

Whatever was or wasn't happening between Michael and Amanda could wait.

This is my night.

TWELVE

Emma Two Hours Ago

In the lonely expanse of the night, Emma's footsteps echoed on the wet pavement, each one a sharp reminder of her solitude. The rain had soaked through her clothes, leaving her chilled to the bone, yet it was the emptiness beside her that left her feeling truly cold.

As she clutched the knife—a last vestige of Angeline's presence—it served as both a comfort and a cruel reminder of her isolation. The night was deep, the darkness almost tangible, as if she could reach out and touch the blackness that enveloped her. Emma knew moving forward was the only option, yet each step seemed heavier, weighed down by the realisation that no matter where she went, Angeline would not be there to meet her.

Tonight, as she wandered towards the bridge that arched gracefully over the river, that turbulent thought churned in the back of her mind.

She would not find Angeline.

No matter how far she retraced their steps, she would not find her.

Angeline would not answer her calls. She would not reply to her texts.

And without Angeline, what was she?
Alone.

She was nothing. Nobody. She was simply alone.

And that wasn't enough.

The bridge loomed ahead, its structure a stark silhouette against the city's dimly lit skyline. It was an old bridge, one that carried countless stories and secrets over its span. Emma and Angeline had always loved it, not just for its architectural beauty, but for the emotional sanctuary it had provided for them on those long nights when the world seemed too much to handle.

Now, as she approached it, the bridge seemed to take on a new role. It was no longer just a pathway over water, but a metaphor for her current state—caught between moving forward and staying anchored to the past. The rain beat down harder as she made her way onto the bridge, the rhythmic pounding on the pavement mirroring the tumult in her heart.

Emma moved forward and walked up the paved incline. The weight of her bag felt heavier than before, each step a testament to the effort of simply existing. The city's lights reflected off the surface of the churning dark water below her, creating a distorted mirror of the world above. The sight of the river, always moving, always flowing, was relentless, indifferent to her pain.

Stopping midway, Emma leaned against the cold, uninviting railing as she had done countless times before with Angeline.

The bridge itself, an elegant span of weathered stone and iron, had always been more than a mere crossing for Emma and Angeline. Its arches were adorned with countless padlocks, each a testament to a promise or a memory cherished by others who had passed this way. Tonight, the padlocks clinked softly in the wind, a haunting melody of the many loves and losses that the bridge bore witness to. It was as if the bridge, in its steadfastness, mocked the fragility of human connections, standing unchanged as the lives of those who had left their marks upon it had moved on, or ended.

Emma ran her hand over the clusters of assorted locks: gold, silver steel, plastic. She couldn't help but wonder about the people that had attached them, and the friends, lovers, or family that they had dedicated them to. Theirs was there, still; the metal untarnished. She let it rest in her hand and thought about the day they had fastened it there, together.

Emma remembered the evening in vivid detail. It had been clear and warm, nothing like the present day. The two of them had been on their usual walk, bathed in the golden hue of the setting sun, when Angeline pulled out the small, brass padlock.

"For us," she had said, showing Emma their initials etched into the metal before they joined hands to click the lock closed on the railing.

"We will always be a part of this place. Just like it's a part of us. Whatever happens, Em, we will always have each other."

Emma had cried then, as she did now, but then it had been for a different, more positive reason.

Angeline palmed the key and threw it into the river below, smiling and reaching to wipe her sister's tears.

"Always," she said, as together they had watched the key sink into the river below.

It was a pledge of eternal sisterhood in the face of the relentless flow of time. But time was cruel. And *always* wasn't anywhere near as long as it should have been.

She was alone.

Behind Emma, cars passed intermittently, their presence more felt than seen in the murky night. Every twenty seconds or so, the hiss of tyres slicing the rain-soaked street, and the low growl of an engine punctuated the otherwise sombre background sounds of the night. Each vehicle's passing was accompanied by a brief gust of air and the distorted reflection of lights, dancing across the wet asphalt, momentarily illuminating Emma's solitary figure before plunging her back into the dim glow of the streetlamps.

The usual throng of lovers, joggers and dreamers had mostly been driven away by the night's foul weather. The only people who passed were hunched against the rain, hurrying past without a glance, wrapped up in their own lives.

Who do I have now?

Who's left to care about me?

There was no one left to care. No one to miss her. All she had were sleepless nights and endless days that felt equally dark.

This place had been the end point of so many walks with Angeline. They would cross the bridge, loop back, and head home. Back through the park, back past Coffee Express, back to their flat. Together. Alone.

This place would be a fitting end point now.

Emma pulled up her sleeve, exposing her pale skin to the elements. The sinew, the blue lines of her veins, the soft inviting flesh were all so familiar to her. Above them, though, was something that made her pause. The tattoo that she and Angeline shared. Same words, same font, same place.

Everything happens for a reason.

It was a line that both of them used to believe.

Her arm was becoming pink in the bitter cold; the black letters still stood out.

Tell me why, then.

Tell me why.

Angeline was a part of her and always would be.

Thrusting a hand into her pocket, she felt again the weight of the knife. Emma clenched her fist around it: it was a perfect fit. Her sister knew her so well.

Angeline was in her veins, and perhaps it was time to cut her out.

The knife wasn't just a means of defence; it was a potential escape, a way out of the pain that seemed to encompass her world. Angeline had given it to her to protect her body, never suspecting it might one day be wielded in a battle against her own spiralling thoughts.

"I wanted to protect you, not hurt you. I would never want you to hurt yourself."

Emma swung her head around, so sure was she that the words had come from a physical presence on the bridge. It was Angeline's voice, unmistakable, that had spoken.

"Angeline?" Emma called out.

A couple, about to walk past her, pulled in more closely to each other, one of the girls flashing her a look as they passed by.

Emma didn't care.

"Angeline," she shouted again.

Her sister was not there.

"Angeline," she said, quietly now, a breath of a word.

She stood, her silhouette etched against the dim glow of the city. Droplets of water found their way around her hood, plastering her hair to her forehead, and tracing meandering paths down her cheeks.

Below, the river was a black abyss, its surface an undulating mirror reflecting the sporadic glimmers of the city lights. The rain, ever persistent, tapped a rhythmic, almost hypnotic pattern, distorting the reflections into a kaleidoscope of broken light. It was a beauty she could recognise, even in her darkest moment. The sound of the water, a soft, continuous murmur, seemed to speak directly to Emma's emotions. It was soothing, despite its choppy churning.

Emma felt the wet wood of the railing under her fingertips; the grain swollen and slick, an anchor to the present.

She breathed in.

The night air was fresh, carrying with it the scent of wet concrete, a deep, earthy aroma that mingled with the faint traces of the city's exhaust and the distant, almost forgotten fragrance of the river's natural musk.

It smelled like life.

Emma filled her lungs with air, and let the breath out again, as though remembering what it was to be alive.

Angeline was not there, but in a way she always would be.

"I'm sorry, Angeline," Emma said.

Reaching deep into her pocket, she drew out the knife.

Pulling her arm back, she threw the gift from her sister with as much force as she could manage over the edge of the bridge into the dark water.

There was someone left to care about her: it was herself.

She had to move forward.

Tonight, she had to say goodbye to Angeline.

As she leant against the barrier, looking down into the turbulent river below, she heard a noise from behind her.

A car stopped.

A man's voice called out.

"Do you need a ride?"

Emma's thoughts were consumed with her sister. Her emotions were too close to the surface.

She span and spat out her reply to the driver.

"Go to hell. Go to hell. Go…"

Emma's voice broke.

The man in the car lifted his hands and rolled his window closed, shutting out Emma and her words.

He sped away, just as quickly as he had arrived.

Emma turned and readied herself to make her way to where she knew she needed to be.

"Angeline, I'm coming," she said. "I'm coming now."

But as she turned to leave, a soft clink caught her attention. With her hood pulled up and the wind blustering, she shouldn't have heard it. The sound was too gentle to be real. But there, glinting under the moonlight, was a new padlock, freshly locked onto the bridge.

Etched upon it were the words, *Always with you, A.*

Emma's breath caught. The padlock's presence was impossible, yet there it was—an undeniable sign that defied logic.

"Everything happens for a reason," Emma whispered.

She traced her finger over the message etched into the metal and then turned to make her way to her final destination.

THIRTEEN

Now

David's hand paused on the gear stick, the distant purr of the engine cutting through the silence. From the corner of his eye, he saw the girl step closer to the car, her posture stiff. She hadn't taken her eyes off the approaching vehicle with its red and blue glow since she had spotted it.

"Police," she stated flatly, her voice barely above a murmur, as though she needed to say something, but didn't know what.

Stating the obvious was fine, but David needed the girl to move.

His throat tightened, the urge to flee wrestling with the need to appear indifferent. He couldn't let the girl see the panic clawing at his insides. He was torn between wanting her to hurry, to get into the car so they could be on their way, and wanting her to take her time so he could compose himself.

His palm was clammy against the leather, and he withdrew his hand, wiping it on the damp fabric of his tux trousers. What must he look like? Soaked to the skin, dressed in this suit, out here with a strange girl.

He took a couple of deep breaths, trying to calm himself, and called out to the girl.

"Are you coming?" he asked, a forced casualness in his tone.

The girl looked as though she was a photograph of herself, blown up to life size. Rigid, unmoving.

"Twenty-One?" he called, trying to keep the tone light even though he felt the heavy weight of the night and his actions upon him.

The words seemed to snap her to life, and she darted to the passenger door.

"We should go," she said, with an urgency in her voice that matched David's own concealed anxiety.

She slid into the passenger seat, placing her legs to either side of the bag in the footwell, and slammed the door.

"We should go," she said again, looking at the driver. "Now."

David checked his mirror out of muscle memory rather than necessity, flicked on the indicator, and sped up along the road.

The car complied with no sign that it had any objection. The damage from the collision was superficial, at least on their end.

As the police car moved towards them, and they towards it, David tried not to think about what might happen if the officer inside pulled them over.

"They've got their lights on," the girl stated the obvious again. She was struggling. "They must be in a hurry. They won't stop."

The two vehicles came level and then glided past each other. As they passed, the distinctive whine of the Doppler effect resonated in David's ears, its pitch bending and fading even through the drumming rain.

"Guess so," he replied. His nonchalance sounded forced, and he tried to dial it down. "They must be on their way back to the crime scene," David said, not taking his eyes off the road.

"What?" the girl said, before quickly following on. "Of course. Her."

She flicked her gaze up to the mirror, but there was no sign of the patrol vehicle. It had already rounded a bend, heading off into the darkness of the night.

"Did you see him look in the car?" the girl asked, as though it was insignificant.

"What?" David started.

"The driver. The policeman. Had a good look."

Her voice was muffled. The girl was rustling in her bag, pulling something out. David wished she would stop. He wished she wasn't there. He wished he had never picked her up. How would he explain to the police what a man like him was doing with a girl like her in the car? How could it look anything other than nefarious or perverse?

"Oh," David said, and left it at that.

The girl had retrieved her phone and was tapping at the screen again. Not the game, this time. David cast a quick look over and saw a string of messages; the girl was typing.

"You got a signal?" he asked.

The girl shook her head.

"Nah." She waved her hand, as if batting him away. "You don't have to watch everything I do, you know."

"Sorry," he said, pursing his lips. He was so used to being told off by Charlotte.

Don't come in my room.

Don't wave at me like that when I'm with my friends.

You're embarrassing.

You're lame.

It was normal though, wasn't it? That was how kids dealt with the difference between them and their parents.

Come to think of it, Amanda said most of the same things.

That was how wives dealt with their husbands.

Some wives.

"Just thought I'd better let someone know where I am," the girl said in a cold deadpan. "In case the police come looking for my body next."

David's foot slipped on the accelerator and the car lurched forwards.

"You *have* got a signal, then?" he snapped.

"Chill," she said. "I'm joking." She paused for a second before continuing. "But you seemed pretty worked up when you saw that police car back there."

David fought to compose himself before responding. He could feel the tension throbbing through his body. He had to let it go.

"You seemed pretty eager to get moving yourself," he said without a shred of emotion.

The girl shrugged. He saw the gesture out of the corner of his eye but felt her movement beside him.

"Listen, it's none of my business, I know. But…*does* anyone know where you are?" David asked, and immediately wished he hadn't.

He didn't want to scare her. Or at least not make her any more afraid than she might already be. She was covering her feelings well. She must have a reason to be out there, on the road, alone. There must be an enormous *why* behind her need to take such risks.

"Uh, yeah," she lied.

The girl clicked her phone closed and settled back into the seat, resting her head against the cold glass of the side window.

"I guess that police officer does now," she said without a smile.

David turned his head towards her. She looked so young, sitting there in the same position that he had seen Charlotte in so many times before. It was the position *she* took when she didn't want to talk anymore.

Not young, although of course she was, but vulnerable. That was the aura she was giving off.

134

She looked like that weak, spindly deer that he had first taken her for.

He was hardly a stag himself. He couldn't judge.

Still, he had to say something. He needed to know more.

"Twenty-One," he began. "Why were you out there, on the road?"

"My car," she said. "I told you."

"Yes, that's what you told me," David replied. "But why *were* you out there on the road?"

A sudden flashback came to him, the instinct he had felt when he first picked her up: she was running from something.

It *was* none of his business, of course, but perhaps he could help. Perhaps he could align the balance of his shit awful night by doing something down-to-earth *good*.

"My car," she said again, mocking her own tone.

It was the only answer he was going to get.

He knew how to take a hint, so he didn't ask again.

"Okay," David sighed. "It's just you and I here, you know. We're never going to see each other again after tonight. If you wanted to talk…"

"If I wanted to talk I…"

She stopped, mid-sentence.

"Oh crap," she said instead.

"What?" David instinctively pressed on the brake.

"No." She said the word instinctively rather than answering his question. "Behind us."

He looked up into the rear-view mirror and he saw it too.

The police car. Pale headlights glowing against the black of the forest road. The red and blue signal blaze coming back towards them, towards him.

He was screwed.

He knew it.

There was no getting out of this.

It was time for the truth to seep out.

Beside him, Twenty-One shifted uneasily, her earlier composure cracking. Whatever her reasons for being out here, it was clear they both had something they preferred to keep hidden from the prying eyes of the law.

Whatever her secret was, though, it couldn't be anywhere near as serious as his.

As the red and blue lights drew closer, painting the night with flickers of urgency, David felt his stomach tighten. The siren blared from the police car, cutting through the background sounds of the night.

He had to stop.

David took a deep breath and eased the car to the side of the road, the sodden dirt soft, forest debris crunching under the tyres; a stark contrast to the silence that fell inside the vehicle.

David and the girl exchanged a quick, tense look—a silent agreement, but to what, he wasn't sure. They were in something together, and at the moment, it felt like that was going to be a shit heap of trouble.

The officer pulled up behind them and stepped out of his vehicle.

The storm seemed to intensify, as if to underscore the gravity of the moment, blurring the windows and distorting the approaching figure of the lone policeman.

"You're shaking," the girl said, nodding towards David's hands, still on the wheel.

He pulled them back towards him, out of view.

"I'm fine," he said, but his voice didn't come out as confidently as he had hoped. "I'm fine," he repeated.

FOURTEEN

David Two Hours Ago

David navigated his way through the elegantly dressed crowd to table number one, his emotions a complex symphony of excitement, nerves, and an irritation that bubbled just beneath the surface. The sight of the empty seat next to his own was a stark reminder of Amanda's absence, a void that seemed to echo louder in the grandeur of the Hall.

Even if she was a homebody, preferring a quiet night in with a book rather than the extravagance of an awards ceremony, she would have played her part tonight. She would have been every bit as elegant and eloquent as Della, every bit as beautiful and more. Amanda wasn't as well educated as most of the other people in the hall, but she knew how to bring the charm; she could talk to anybody, and she usually did. Many times he had been left, sitting beside her, listening to her talk for hours with his coworkers, his family, and on those rare occasions he met with them, his friends.

He, on the other hand, had the kind of awkwardness in starting conversations that left him feeling that his tongue was two sizes too large for his mouth. Amanda helped to ease him into small talk. Much as he hated it, he knew it was necessary. He didn't enjoy anything that made him feel like a failure.

Amanda not being there with him was one of those things.

He couldn't let his feelings show. Not in front of Michael. Not now. Not ever. Instead, he settled into his seat with a practiced smile, attempting to mask the cocktail of emotions.

At the table, Michael's laughter was already too loud, his demeanour too self-assured. As David settled into his seat, Michael was seemingly embroiled in a bout of bonhomie with the two colleagues and their partners, who had drawn the short straw of sharing their table. Della, ever the embodiment of grace, offered David a sympathetic smile, which he returned with a nod. Around them, their coworkers at the surrounding tables engaged in idle chatter, their voices a background hum to David's tumultuous thoughts.

Of course, Michael would be there first. In the time it had taken David to walk across the room, Michael and Della had already settled into their places. They looked comfortable. Even Michael was relaxed and calm beneath his laughter.

"Made it to the top table, eh? Big night, David," Michael finally acknowledged David's arrival. He leaned in, his voice tinged with a familiarity that grated. "Nervous?"

David offered a tight smile. He would not give Michael the satisfaction, especially not when Michael showed no sign of anxiety. Some people thrived in crowds, and anyway, Michael wasn't the one who was going to need to stand up there and speak in front of two hundred colleagues.

"It's an honour just to be nominated," he replied, the rehearsed line feeling hollow in his own ears.

"I have to say, Burny, I was hoping I'd be sitting next to your delightful wife rather than you this evening. I feel like we have, I don't know, more in common, maybe?"

"It's lucky you have your own *delightful* wife, isn't it?" David said, trying to tone down the venom in his voice.

Della raised her eyebrows, looking to Michael for a reaction, and that was enough for David. He wanted to know that she was listening to her husband's taunts. If Michael wanted to throw any mud around, some of it was going to stick on him, too.

Was there something going on between Michael and Amanda?

The thought, once ludicrous, began to take root in the fertile ground of David's agitation. With every knowing look Michael shot in his direction, the idea grew. He knew Michael and Amanda spoke to each other, sure. They met every time she bothered to come to the stuffy work functions, and

140

he had seen the connection between them. But everyone loved Amanda. Attractive, charming, sweet Amanda. Or at least that's what you'd think if you hadn't been married to her for twenty years.

All the times he had heard Michael and Amanda laughing together, had they actually been laughing at him?

And what was it Charlotte had said?

David reached out for his glass and almost took a gulp of the champagne. He pulled up short and held the stem between his fingers. It was smooth, fragile. It could break so easily.

"In a world of your own, tonight, aren't you?" Michael said, reaching under the table and giving him an insalubrious pat on the thigh.

David jerked his leg and pulled his arm back towards his body in a simultaneous reflex action. Some of the champagne splashed out onto the white linen tablecloth, leaving pale yellow bubbles on the surface.

"Alright, mate. I wasn't trying to feel you up."

Michael withdrew and shook his head.

He pities me.

David couldn't shake the thought.

He pities me, but tonight I'm going home with the award. I'm going home to Amanda.

"Just a little nervous," David laughed, buoyed by the realisation that despite whatever Michael felt about him, he was the winner. He was the better man.

Michael smiled back.

The hall fell silent as the ceremony began. When Malcolm gave his opening speech, David tried to concentrate, but his mind flitted between Amanda, the upcoming award, and the speech he was still not confident about delivering. Each minor trophy handed out was dispensed with polite applause and broad smiles from office workers David only knew in passing. Most Improved Worker, Team Innovation Award, Sustainability Champion. What did any of those things even mean? The accolades were unimportant to David: stepping stones to the moment that truly mattered.

Amid the formalities, there was a break in Michael's banter. He sat silent, formal, and reverent as the small plaques and handshakes were distributed. Rookie of the Year. Best Remote Worker. Mitchell joked the recipient wasn't able to come in to receive the award, creating a ripple of polite laughter around the room. David forced his own response and wished for the awarding of trivial trophies to be over.

He looked across at Michael, but instead caught Della's eye. She gave him a small silent nod, and a purse-lipped smile. Della was beautiful, but at that moment, she looked so very tired.

David tried to focus on the ceremony, on the recognition he was sure was imminent, but Michael's words were like spectres at the edge of his consciousness, impossible to ignore completely. He scrolled through his mental recollection of everything Michael had said, just as Charlotte scrolled through her damn phone. Every mention of Amanda, every shared chuckle over past memories, felt deliberate, a subtle chiselling away at the foundations of David's composure. The laughter and nods across the table might as well have been daggers, each one embedding seeds of doubt and suspicion deeper into David's thoughts. As dull as the opening prize-giving was, at least it had shut Michael's mouth.

Finally, the moment arrived.

Malcolm Mitchell, Tursten Mitchell's venerable CEO, stood centre stage with the grace of a seasoned conductor ready to direct the night's climax. The envelope he held was not just paper; it was a vessel of David's hopes, the tangible manifestation of years of dedication and dreams. In his other hand, he held aloft the award, for all to see. It was beautiful, and it was about to be in David's hands. The chandelier lights above reflected off the angular glass trophy; it shone like a beacon.

David was doubtlessly romanticising the moment, but this was the big one. This was the most important night of his life. His feelings were a tempest of anticipation and nerves, as Malcolm Mitchell gave his preamble.

"…given more than any other to this company…"

The heat within David intensified as the CEO spoke. The silence in the hall was electric, every attendee holding their breath in collective anticipation. David's future, he felt, hung in the balance of the imminent revelation.

"…someone I know I can always turn to…"

His cheeks glowed. His legs felt tension-sprung, ready to stand and make his way to the stage.

"…a born leader. I'm proud to think of the recipient of this award as a friend, not just an employee…"

He suddenly knew exactly what he was going to say when he stood beside Mitchell. Everything was clear. This was it. He felt a rush. A flood of emotion rushed through David's body. He looked around the room, hoping to see his colleagues looking back. All eyes were focussed on Mitchell. He wanted to be on the stage with him. He wanted the recognition now, now, now.

He was ready.

Mitchell made a show of opening the envelope in his hand, resting the trophy down on the podium while he did so. There was no list of nominees to read out. There was no doubt who the winner would be.

Mitchell spoke, his words echoing in the silent room.

"And the award goes to… Michael Johnson."

The sentence fell like a guillotine, severing David's hopes with a finality that left him momentarily breathless. The room erupted into applause, a cacophony that drowned out the rush of blood in David's ears, the sound of his own heart fracturing under the weight of disappointment and disbelief.

Michael's hand fell onto his shoulder, too heavy, too hard. It was crushing.

David opened his mouth, but no words came out.

Michael looked at him, his expression one of smug satisfaction. To his side, Della rose, and he turned to her, giving her a long, smooching kiss that sent the onlooking crowd into uproarious laughter. Michael's hand was still resting on David's tux jacket.

"Time for that later, Johnson," Malcolm Mitchell laughed along from the stage. "Come and get this bloody award before I drop it."

Michael broke from the kiss and patted David like a dog before walking towards the waiting CEO.

As he made his way, colleagues that David didn't even know stopped Michael, reaching out to shake his hand. One stood to pat him on the shoulder and ended up giving him an awkward hug that sent a roar of laughter around the room. Michael's victory parade to the stage was a blur, his triumphant glee a visible aura that seemed to fill the space with an unbearable lightness.

David clapped along with the rest, the action mechanical, divorced from the turmoil that churned within. Each clap was a mockery, a salute to the dismantling of his aspirations, to the triumph of a man he could no longer view merely as a colleague but as a usurper, a thief of more than just an award.

He was sandwiched now between two empty seats. One had belonged to Michael. The other, the chair where Amanda should have been, was a chasm, a physical representation of the absence he felt more acutely now in his moment of defeat. What would Amanda have said if she had been there? He wanted to pull out his phone and text her – no, phone her – there and then. He wanted her to know how he had been betrayed.

But the seeds of suspicion Michael had sown throughout the evening had taken root in this fertile ground of betrayal and loss, intertwining with his professional disappointment to form a knot of emotions David could scarcely begin to untangle. Perhaps she would tell him that, of course, Michael deserved to win. Of course, he was the better employee, the better man.

Every thought David had as he watched Michael stride up to take the award was filled with hatred.

As though sensing his seething disappointment, though it was written clearly on his face, Della reached across to touch David's hand; he tugged it away.

"No," he hissed. "Don't."

Della stared at him with cool indifference. She was playing a role. She was Michael's wife.

And he was the winner.

FIFTEEN

Now

The officer walked slowly, his silhouette a shadow against the backdrop of the patrol car's flashing lights. Pausing by the window, his hat brim dripping with rainwater, he held a flashlight in his hand that he didn't immediately use.

The car's interior light flicked on automatically as David rolled down the window, casting them in a harsh, unforgiving glow. The rain tapped incessantly against the car, an irregular drumbeat underscoring the unfolding scene.

"Evening," the policeman called out through the sound of the rainfall, his voice betraying a hint of weariness. "Sorry to stop you folks on a night like this. We're checking all vehicles coming from the direction of Maplewood. There's been an incident."

David nodded; his throat tight. "Of course, officer. How can we help?"

"Have you seen anything unusual out here tonight?"

David shook his head without missing a beat.

"Nothing," he said. "We haven't seen anything."

He could feel the tremor in his voice still. Not as severe as when he had answered the girl, but present all the same.

148

Calm down.
Calm down.
Calm down.

"Any other cars on the road? Anyone acting in a way that might have caught your attention?"

David looked at the girl. Her face was a mask of cool boredom.

"Nothing," he said again, pacing himself this time. "We hadn't seen a single vehicle until we saw you heading that way."

The policeman nodded.

"Do you know why I came back?"

David shook his head. The officer had just told him they were checking all vehicles, and all vehicles, from what he had seen, added up to only his. Still, he wasn't going to make any wild statements. He wasn't going to say anything that might incriminate him. He said nothing.

"Because the boss told me to," the officer half-smiled. His face snapped back to solemnity as he continued. "A body was found earlier this evening." He spoke the words in a semi-whisper, as though trying to protect the girl's innocent young ears from such horror.

"We heard," David said. "On the radio."

The officer looked into the car, his eyes focussing on the car stereo, as though checking David's claim. It was humming out a background buzz of bland pop music, but the officer nodded at it as though that was a solid enough corroboration.

"There are no immediate witnesses as yet. The boss wondered whether you might have noticed anything. Back there."

"Nothing," David repeated. "I'm sorry we couldn't be of more help. It sounds terrible."

He didn't want to sound either interested or disinterested. He would try to throw together a story, should the officer ask. Again, he wished he had planned ahead, but tonight was a night he hadn't expected. There were so many variables that he would never have thought of factoring in.

The policeman nodded, disappointment and resignation merging in his expression.

"Okay," he said. "If you think of anything later that might be useful…"

David returned the nod. "Of course," he said. "I'll call it in."

The officer tilted his head and made a sound like he was sucking air through his teeth. As if an afterthought, he shone his flashlight into the car.

"What brings you out here so late at night?" he asked. His voice was different, somehow, as though he was asking something he might actually get an answer to rather than chasing up a lead because he'd been told to.

David's imagination whirred into action, prompted by the inescapable question.

The officer feigned focus upon David, but his eyes darted into the car in a way that seemed so natural he must have done the same thing countless times before. He scanned the interior. The girl. The backseats. David.

David paused.

Think, think, think.

"I…"

"It's my fault," the girl cut in. "The officer won't care, Dad," she said, talking to him. "It's okay."

David swallowed hard, trying to mask his surprise. He made the split-second decision to trust the girl, let her go with it.

"I had a row with Mum," she said, turning her eyes down as though embarrassed. "She caught me smoking again, and she went off the scale nuts. I…I ran out of the house. In this…" The girl gestured at the rain that was bouncing off the policeman's jacket. "Dad came after me."

Dad.

Okay.

David joined in the pretence.

"I wanted to take her straight back," David improvised. "But Amanda, my wife, her mum…well, you know how women get sometimes."

The officer gave David a piercing stare. David changed tack. His line was going to be received one way or the other, and unfortunately for him, it had fallen against him. He worked to bring the policeman back on side.

"Probably just the women that have to put up with living with me then," he smiled, patting the girl on the leg.

Rather than pull away, the girl put her hand on top of David's and wrapped her fingers around his. It felt simultaneously comforting and unnerving.

"We weren't going anywhere, really," David said. "It was a drive to cool off, you know. For Amanda to cool off, anyway. My wife."

"You've said, yes. And do you think she might have *cooled off* by now?" The policeman pronounced the words in a mock repetition of David's tone.

"Not yet," the girl laughed. David could tell that she was trying to ease the tension in the conversation, and he relaxed his hand in appreciative acknowledgement.

The policeman made a sharp humming sound. He sounded tired, or at least tired of having to stand in the rain asking questions.

"And sir, Mr…?"

"David," David said. "David Burnham. Do you need to see my license?"

The officer waved the suggestion away.

"No, Mr Burnham, but I have a few more questions for you."

David's pulse skipped, and he tried to keep his composure.

"Do you always dress like this, when you're sitting at home, waiting for your daughter and wife to stop arguing?"

"What?" David's voice caught in his throat.

The girl let out a shrill laugh and nudged David gently in the ribs.

"Oh," David said. "I was at an awards ceremony earlier. For work." He had already given his name. The cop could easily trace his registration and find out exactly where he had been anyway. He just had to hope that it wasn't as simple for the officer to find out what he had done.

"Oh, one of those," the policeman snorted with derision. "Hate them."

"Same," David said, honestly. "I hadn't been home long. You know, when…"

"When your wife and daughter…yes, yes. Okay." The officer looked over at the girl, and then back at David. "Fine, fine."

David had almost let himself relax when the next question came.

"And before," the policeman said, changing direction, "When I saw you. You were in the middle of the road. You stopped for some reason. Why was that?"

David's mind raced. It mustn't have looked good. The car parked in the middle of the road. On a busy day, it would have been a hazard. With the low visibility tonight, if anyone else had driven along, it could have still ended in disaster.

He wasn't thinking; he wasn't concentrating.

Concentrate now.

Tell the truth.

"I hit a deer," David said, factually, trying to keep his voice steady.

"That was my fault too," the girl said. "I was crying, and Dad - just for a split second - looked at me. And it was there. It ran out, you know." The girl waved her arms as if it helped the explanation. "He's really careful. It wasn't his fault. Please don't be mad at him because of me."

The officer nodded at the girl and turned his attention back to David. David jumped to the snap conclusion that the policeman was a father. The cop seemed to understand the girl, but then, as a father himself, David understood so little.

"You didn't see the sign then?" the officer asked. "The sign with a picture of a deer on it? You remember your Highway Code, of course, sir?"

Even if he didn't, the meaning was easy to decipher.

"I did. I was driving quite slowly, with the rain and all."

Another truth. David felt a warm satisfaction despite his fluttering heart rate. He wanted to add that there was no way he could have avoided the accident, that even if he had seen it coming, there was nothing he could have done to stop it, but he kept his thoughts to himself.

The policeman repeated his bored low humming noise.

"Okay, sir," he said. "I'm just going to take a look at your vehicle."

"It's fine, really," David said sharply. "I've already been out to check it over. There's a tiny dent, that's all."

"You own the vehicle?" the officer asked.

"Company," David said. "It's registered in my name, though."

The officer narrowed his eyes and shone his torch into the car again, scanning the backseats as though searching for something.

"Sir, I'm going to ask you to step out of the vehicle, and we are going to look over your car."

"We?"

"You and I, sir," the policeman explained.

David felt a knot in his stomach.

If he carried on arguing with the officer, it would only raise suspicion. He wanted this over with, now. In a brief moment of altruistic thought, he wished he could tell the girl to go, to run, to get away. How, though? Out here, where he had come to hide, he realised that there was nowhere to hide at all.

He looked at Twenty-One and patted her leg.

"I won't be long," he said. "You stay here. Look after yourself." He stressed the final words as if trying to give her a secret message. If shit goes down, look out for yourself. Don't worry about me.

"Okay," she said, and looked at him in the same simple way that Charlotte would have. Like he was an embarrassment.

And he was.

He was.

With that, he pushed open the car door and made his way to where the policeman was now shining his torch over the dented front bumper.

He wished for his umbrella, but that was still in the trunk. There was no way he could get it now.

The policeman pointed the flashlight at David's face, causing two bright yellow circles to burst into his vision. He flicked the beam sharply towards the car, as if to spotlight the girl.

"Your daughter then?" the officer said.

They were out of earshot. The girl was staring at them through the window, but unless she could lip read, their conversation was private.

"Yes," David said, without skipping a beat. "Charlotte. I call her Lottie."

"Hmm," the officer frowned. "And a row with the mother?"

David tried not to replicate the frown, but it was difficult, the rain trying again to soak through his suit.

His outfit wasn't helping, he was sure. Who dressed like this? He was pretty sure the answer wasn't casual criminals and murderers, at least.

"They seem to clash a lot now she's getting older."

"How old?" the officer asked, nodding again at the car.

"Nineteen," David answered, again without pause. The girl's story seemed viable. He was throwing himself into it.

"If I give your wife a call, would she corroborate this?"

"She would," David said, more calmly than he felt. "But she would be pissed at me for letting you wake her up."

He attempted a smile, but it seemed there was nothing that could make the officer show any emotion other than annoyance or boredom.

"Okay, sir. I'm sure that won't be necessary. Let's just check your car is okay and you can be on your way."

David internalised the relief he felt.

"Thank you," he said flatly.

The officer nodded towards the damage caused by the impact and then turned to David.

"Must have been a young stag," he said. "You're lucky."

He spoke as though this was something he saw all the time, like city folk made a habit of driving up into the hills and smashing into the native animals.

"Have you seen this?" the officer asked, standing up and moving towards David.

Instinctively and perhaps stupidly, David stepped back.

"It's okay," the officer said. "Look."

He was holding out a thick mat of fur, highlighting it in the beam of his torch.

David felt vomit rise in his throat and swallowed it back. Something about the smell of blood coming from the dense clump turned his stomach. It was a rich metallic odour; it smelled like death.

"Definitely a deer," he said, as if there had been some doubt.

The two of them stood awkwardly, the officer protected by his hat, David exposed. He wanted to get back in the car. He wanted to leave.

The officer's radio crackled to life, and the man raised his hand and stepped away from David and the car.

The incessant rain and the distance that the policeman had put between them made it impossible for David to pick up any of what was being said. David looked through the windshield into the car's interior. The girl was sitting bolt upright, picking at the skin on her nail beds.

"Sir, thank you for your time," the policeman said, clipping his radio back onto his jacket. "I'm afraid there has been a development and I am going to have to leave you now."

"Development?" David asked, as the words filtered their way slowly into his brain.

The officer was leaving. That was the main headline.

"Yes, sir. I'm not at liberty to disclose any further information, but I advise you to take another route and make your way back home now. If you head along to the..."

"I know the roads, officer," David nodded. "I need to stop for fuel up ahead. I don't suppose you noticed if the truck stop is open?"

"It was when I passed," the policeman said, unfazed. "Go straight there, then take your daughter home. Help her patch things up with her mum."

"I will," David said.

The policeman patted David gently on the arm and turned to leave.

As the officer walked away, David let himself breathe out all the tension that he had been carrying within his body. Just as he leant forward, hands reaching out onto the car to steady himself, the policeman spun around.

David jerked to a standing position, his heart almost stopping.

"Sir," the officer called over.

"Yes?" David said in as calm a tone as he could manage.

"Keep driving safely." The policeman didn't wait for a response. Instead, he continued to walk towards his car, quickening his pace.

"I will," David said again.

David climbed back into the driver's seat and let out a sigh that he had been holding in.

"What did he say to you out there?" the girl asked.

David turned to look at her.

"Just checking we weren't out here d-o-g-g-i-n-g," he said, with no hint of emotion.

The girl playfully swung at him with a spindly but surprisingly forceful arm.

"If you told me you knew ju-jitsu, I wouldn't make such terrible jokes," David smiled, batting her away.

She was his daughter's age. It wasn't an appropriate comment, he knew, but she was *not* his daughter. She had, though, covered for him. He just didn't know why.

SIXTEEN

David Two Hours Ago

Della withdrew her hand and turned back to watch her husband. David couldn't take his eyes off Michael, who now stood at the podium with a grin that seemed to stretch from ear to ear. The CEO, Malcolm Mitchell, handed over the trophy with a joviality that grated on every nerve in David's body. The clink of glass against Michael's wedding band as the award transferred hands sounded like a gavel falling, finalising the judgment on David's years of dedication.

As Michael began his acceptance speech, the words seemed to echo mockingly in David's ears.

"I'm truly humbled," Michael proclaimed, his voice resonating through the hall, "and honestly surprised. I haven't been with Tursten Mitchell long, but it feels like family. A place where hard work is recognised and rewarded."

The underlying message, whether or not intentional, felt like a direct affront to David, a denial of all the years he had given to the company.

He had been saving Tursten Mitchell's arse since before Michael Johnson was even hired. He carried his team, working every damn hour to make sure targets were met and clients were happy.

He had made apologies to Amanda for nights he couldn't be with her, skipped holidays he didn't have time to take. Hell, he had even missed Charlotte's eighteenth birthday for the company that was throwing him under the bus.

What had Michael ever sacrificed?

David had given his life.

For nothing.

Tursten Mitchell felt like family to Michael, did it? Tursten Mitchell had taken the place of David's family.

He could feel the blood running to his face, the anger pulsing through his veins.

Around him, colleagues clapped, some rising to their feet, swept up in the ceremony's momentum. Not one of them turned to look at David, to see how he was reacting. It was as though Michael had been meant to win all along. David's hands clapped mechanically, the sound hollow to his own ears. He felt detached, as if observing the scene from outside himself, the pain and betrayal carving a hollow in his chest.

On the stage, in front of all their colleagues, Michael's words continued to flow. There was a stream of gratitude for the team, some hyperbole about the opportunities ahead and the challenges overcome. With each sentence, David felt the gap widen between what he had believed his career at Tursten Mitchell was and what it had apparently become. Michael's casual mention of *innovative directions* and *exciting new ventures to come* under his lead was a bitter pill, implying a future that had no need for David's expertise or experience.

Michael would squash him like a bug after tonight.

David knew it.

He was inferior. Second. Spare.

And he was damned if he was going to stay on working at Tursten Mitchell beneath the smug bastard on the stage.

David's decision was spontaneous and immutable. He had to leave. He had to leave this room, and he had to leave the company.

Rather than feeling like a bullet to the heart, it felt like a key turning in a lock, releasing him from a prison he hadn't realised he was in.

The applause finally ebbed as Michael concluded his speech. The last lines were drowned in the enthusiastic cheers of the crowd. David's applause faltered and finally stopped as he sat back, the feeling of invisibility engulfing him. It was as if the lights, the people, the very air in the room conspired to erase his presence. No matter. He would soon be gone.

Della's concern had turned to a polite mask, her earlier attempt to comfort him abandoned. She was, after all, Michael's wife, bound to share in *his* triumph, not in David's quiet devastation. All he had was the space where Amanda should have been.

He was alone.

In this room full of people, he was truly alone.

As Michael stepped down from the stage, holding the angular glass trophy aloft, David wanted to fade out of existence. He could already presage the torrent that would flow from Michael when he arrived back at the table. Should he go now, before Michael returned?

David inhaled deeply and resolved to stay put. At least for now. One thing was obvious to him, though. Michael had known. He must have known.

There was no way that receiving the award could have come as a surprise. The protracted speech was fluent and well scripted. His demeanour all night had been calm. There was none of the agitation of uncertainty. David cursed himself for not having recognised the signs.

Malcolm Mitchell's voice, lauding Michael's achievements, seemed to come from afar, the words floating over a sea of murmured conversation and smiling faces from which David felt disconnected. The accolade, once a beacon of validation, now cast a shadow over his entire career, over his very sense of self.

Even now, as Michael made his way through the crowd, back to his seat, the CEO continued to heap on the praise, encouraging the crowd to renew their applause.

Enough.

Surely that's enough?

David stared at Mitchell, and the man met his gaze. The CEO's expression was unreadable, a mask as polite as Della's, offering no clue to his motives. Mitchell had surely known that David expected to win the award. How had he chosen Michael over him, disregarding years of loyalty and hard work?

The urge to confront his boss, to demand answers, surged within David, a tide of anger and wounded pride. Yet, the reality of the situation—the public setting, the eyes of colleagues and competitors upon them—forced him to swallow the bitter pill of defeat in silence. What was he going to do? Rush the stage and make a scene in front of Michael's adoring onlookers? David had thought this was *his* night, but it wasn't. It was Michael's night, and loathe as he was to accept that, there was nothing he could do.

Not here. Not now.

He would leave, and Mitchell would miss him.

He would realise, when David was gone, who really put in the work for the company.

But by then it would be too late.

Michael returned to the table, his award in hand. David's smile was a well-crafted facade, a shield against the humiliation and the growing suspicion of betrayal. The evening, once a symbol of hope and recognition, had turned into a picture of defeat and doubt.

Michael bent and waved the trophy in David's face.

It was undeniably beautiful. A six-inch diamond-cut glass plaque.

The name MICHAEL JOHNSON was engraved in upper case serif font, above the words Tursten Mitchell Lifetime Achievement. The company logo sat neatly below to complete the simple design.

Plain, to the point, and undeserved.

"Pretty sweet, huh?" Michael asked him, as he dipped down to Della and kissed her full on the lips.

"Looks like a health and safety violation waiting to happen," David snided, reaching out to put his finger on one of the angular points. He drew it back in feigned alarm.

Michael laughed and set the award down on the table between the two of them.

"When I'm CEO, I'll make sure we ban this kind of thing completely," Michael smiled. "You're right. Dangerous. Definitely out of order. But then..." He paused, and whispered, "You'll never get one, will you, Burny?"

David tried to fake another grin, but it felt like an impossible task.

"People always get what they deserve," he said flatly.

Michael looked his colleague dead in the eye, silent for a long moment, and then burst out into a peal of hysterical laughter.

"I love this guy," he said, turning back to Della.

Della smiled, first at her husband and then, with less feeling, at David.

She was doing her best.

Amanda, on the other hand, wasn't there to do anything. Not to support him in his success, or in what had turned out to be his defeat.

The empty seat beside David served as a stark reminder of his solitude - Amanda's absence mirroring his sense of abandonment by the company he had loyally served for over a decade. It underscored the void that had opened up within him, a void filled with disillusionment and bitter disappointment. The accolade he had expected, which had seemed so within reach, had slipped through his fingers, awarded to a man whose time with the company was but a fraction of his own.

"Got to go and mingle, Burny," Michael said with another inane smile. "Look after Del for me."

He kissed his wife again, and then he scooped the trophy from the table and headed out into the crowd.

As David sat between the empty chairs, the reality of the evening's events slowly sank in. The joviality and laughter around him felt like a harsh contrast to the cold emptiness settling in his chest. The ceremony had moved on, but for David, time seemed to stand still, each passing moment deepening his sense of alienation. He realised with painful clarity that his view of his place within Tursten Mitchell had been fundamentally altered. What he had perceived as a career defined by dedication and achievement was now tainted by the stark revelation of his overlooked contributions.

Tonight was not his night.

He had been wrong.

And now he was going to leave.

"Do you mind if I…? Will you be okay?" he asked Della, in the sheepish tone of a boy asking to slip away to the toilet, not an adult man making his excuses to quit a hideous, painful party.

Della gave him her Mona Lisa smile one more time.

"I'll be fine," she said. "Will you?"

David pulled a tight-lipped grin.

"Of course," he said. "Congratulations to Michael. He's done a lot for the company."

He couldn't think of a single thing that his colleague had done that he personally hadn't done better, but wasn't there a saying about being humble in victory and gracious in defeat? Michael was anything but humble, but David wasn't Michael.

Still, he had been defeated. He felt it in every fibre of his body.

168

When David finally stood, the room seemed to spin slightly, the laughter and voices around him blending into a cacophony that seemed distant and alien.

He nodded to Della, seemingly blissful in her own solitude, and slipped away.

No one watched him.

No one cared.

He would go home, back to Amanda and Charlotte. The evening together would have mollified them; they would be peaceful and content, and soon he would too.

No more competition, no more fighting.

His future was with his family.

Or at least that's what David thought.

SEVENTEEN

Now

David watched the officer's retreating figure blend into the wash of rain and glowing headlights, each step easing the vice of tension that had been gripping his chest. He took a moment, letting the cool air fill his lungs, the rain mingling with the sweat on his brow, a baptism of sorts in the night's chill. Then, with a heavy sigh, he turned back to the car, the reality of their precarious situation settling back onto his shoulders.

As he slid back into the driver's seat, the girl gave him a scrutinising look. Her fingers had stopped their nervous dance around her nail beds, and she seemed more composed, almost relieved.

"We need to talk," David said, his voice low as he started the engine again. "Back there... what you did—stepping in like that. Thanks."

She nodded, a flicker of a smile brushing her lips before disappearing into the stoic mask she had been wearing since the officer left.

"It's fine. But you're right. We should talk. That will be fun. We should also keep moving."

David turned towards her, swivelling in his seat. The cloying scent of artificial vanilla cupcake hit him full on as his body faced the girl.

He said nothing. He looked at her, and she at him.

Eventually, he asked, "Why?"

"Hmm?" the girl responded.

"Why did you lie to the policeman?" It wasn't the question he most wanted to hear the answer to, but it was a good place to start. "Back there, with the officer..." he repeated, his voice rough with the effort of speaking. "Why did you cover for me?"

She turned to look at him, her face a mask of calm that didn't quite reach her eyes. "You looked like you needed a break," she said simply, a shrug accompanying her words as if to say that her actions required no deeper explanation.

"But why?" He pressed, needing to understand, to find some logic in the night's chaos.

"Because sometimes," she drawled, her gaze fixed on the road ahead, "the person running the hardest is the one who needs the most help. And maybe because I know what it's like to wish someone would cover for me."

David absorbed her words, the resonance of their shared desperation settling heavily in the car.

"Listen, I don't know why you really are out here, but I saw the look on your face when that police car showed up, and I saw how you nearly crapped your pants when it stopped behind us..."

"Maybe I just don't like police," David said.

"Maybe you just don't like police," the girl conceded. "Or maybe you aren't heading anywhere at all. Maybe you're running away from something."

Again, David was silent.

"Look at you." She pointed up to the mirror, as though she meant the words literally as well as figuratively. "You're wearing a damn tux in the rain, for God's sake. You've been to a party. Alone. You haven't been drinking. I can tell that. But you still look shaken and stirred, Mr David. That policeman was dumb to believe my story. Like you were just sitting around the house dressed like that? Any normal person would have changed straight away." She blurted out a laugh that sounded young, playful.

David did turn his eyes to his reflection. She was right, of course. He should have taken off his jacket, unfastened his prissy tie. If it wasn't for the rain and the fact that he would otherwise have had no protection from it, perhaps he would have done so.

But a tux and a tie didn't make him look like a criminal, did it?

And if he had been home, would he have changed? He would have had a double shot of espresso and tried to work out how the hell to tell Amanda that he was quitting his job. He would have been sitting in the damn suit until he stripped for bed.

Perhaps he didn't fit the mould of 'any normal person'.

"I *was* at an awards ceremony, and now I'm going…"

Where was he going? Away. That wasn't going to hold up anymore.

"Maybe I needed some time alone," he said.

"You are full of maybes, and short on truths," she replied, as though quoting a song she'd heard somewhere. For all he knew, she was.

David stared at himself a moment longer, and then turned back to the girl. She hadn't answered his question. Again, she had turned everything around on him.

"Well, that makes two of us," he said, his voice as cold as the night.

The girl pressed her lips together and raised her eyebrows.

"Maybe you're just like my daughter after all," David said, but he knew as the words came out that they were untrue. Or he hoped to hell that they were.

She threw a look in his direction.

"This is all very sweet," she said. "But I don't need a father figure. You can cut all the comparisons, okay?"

David switched his attention from the road to the girl, and then quickly back again.

"I touched a nerve, didn't I? I'm sorry. I'm not trying to be anything to you. Jeez, it's probably me that needs a daughter figure. Hell knows I've screwed up enough with the real one." The honesty in David's voice felt refreshing, despite the context of their conversation.

He had initially stopped for the girl out of an instinctive, paternal impulse—a knee-jerk reaction honed by years of failed attempts to connect with his Lottie. Maybe it was easier to play guardian to a stranger than to face the tangled emotions waiting at home. A knot tightened in his stomach with the realisation that here he was, potentially failing another young woman who needed him tonight.

He was in no position to be helping anyone. He should have kept driving rather than risk everything by picking up an unnecessary problem.

That was the truth, but every time his mind strayed along its path, he turned away. Whatever he had done, somewhere within him was a decency that he couldn't ignore.

The girl stared at him as though she didn't know how to respond. Rather than making him uncomfortable, it made him feel responsible somehow, for something. He just wasn't sure what.

"I didn't mean to make things weird," David said. His voice carried a weariness that mirrored the dreariness of the night. "Listen," he said with cool resignation. "Let's get on to the truck stop. I need petrol, and a strong coffee. You need to phone someone to come and get you."

Now the girl spoke.

"You want to get rid of me?" she said with a mock pout.

"I think it might be better if you call someone to fix your car, or give you a lift home, maybe. This thing here, you and me...I shouldn't have picked you up. Okay? I was trying to do the right thing, but...I shouldn't have."

She reverted to the sullen stare that he was getting used to. He didn't need to look at her; he could feel her eyes boring into him.

"Shouldn't have? Did you hear what the policeman said?" she asked, her voice a flat tone that didn't match her words. "There was an incident."

"Yes, and you heard what the radio said. We both heard it," David agreed. "But..."

There was no but. He couldn't wish her out there in the dark, danger of the moorland night. He had done what was right, and here she was.

"I'm sorry," he said. "I didn't mean..."

He flicked a quick look in her direction.

"So, what are you going to do? You can't just leave me out there. When we get to the truck stop. You can't throw me out and make me someone else's problem. I helped you back then. I covered for you, and this is how you're going to repay me?"

The deluge of words fell heavily upon David's ears.

"You're *not* a problem. I didn't mean that. You have someone you can call, don't you?"

The girl didn't answer. David was uncertain whether the silence was the typical sulking he was used to from Charlotte, or whether her stare meant that there *was* no one, that she was also on her own in whatever trouble she was in.

What he did know, though, was that she was a young girl, a young woman, as Lottie would have reminded him. Whatever happened, he really couldn't ditch her.

"I won't leave you alone, okay? I'll stay with you until someone comes out to help you. That's the best I can do."

The girl raised her hands. It was no kind of answer, but it would have to do.

The wipers rhythmically sliced through the rain, each swipe clearing the windshield only for it to be immediately blurred again. The cabin of the car was thick with the tension of unspoken thoughts, the air almost palpable with the secrets they carried. David felt the weight of the evening pressing down on him, a cloak of guilt and regret that was as suffocating as the damp tuxedo clinging to his skin.

He thought about speaking, but didn't know any words that would fit the situation. He wasn't even sure what the situation was anymore.

Each time an insipid pop song ended on the radio, his nerves were on edge, expecting the announcer to break in with a new update. So far, though, there had been nothing.

There had also, he noted with relief, been no further police cars passing. Most of the force had probably been tucked up at home with their own delightful families before being called out to the scene of the incident. Their officer must have come from the other side of the hills, or maybe he had been up at the truck stop emptying the coffee machine of its last shots.

As they drove onwards, he was no doubt making that irritating humming sound whilst talking to his colleagues. They probably –

The girl's voice cut through David's thoughts.

"You said you were at an awards ceremony," the girl said, out of nowhere. She had been leaning against the window again for the past few wordless miles. "That's quite the occasion to end up… here."

David grimaced; the memory of the evening's promise turned nightmare twisted in his gut. This was what the girl had been thinking about, sitting there in her bubble of silence? Why not talk about it then? Or at least some of it.

"It was supposed to be my night," he confessed, his voice a low growl of resentment and bitterness. He didn't even try to hide it. What was the point now? "A recognition of all the years I've given them. But…"

His voice trailed off; the end of that sentence was too grim to voice aloud.

"Instead, here you are, driving in the rain with a stranger," she filled in quietly, her tone not mocking but strangely empathetic. "Running from what should have been a celebration. You are running, aren't you?"

David glanced at her, the dashboard lights illuminating her features in brief flashes. There was an understanding in her eyes that unnerved him, a look that suggested she knew more about fleeing from the past than he cared to ask.

"Everyone is running from something," he said after a moment, the words feeling truer than he intended. "Tonight, it just so happens we're both running in the same direction."

Her laugh was soft, almost inaudible over the storm, but it was there—a dark, melodic sound that hinted at her own familiarity with escape.

"Maybe that's all life is," she mused, "a series of escapes from moments that don't turn out the way we hope."

David felt a chill that had nothing to do with the rain seeping into his bones. "You sound like you've had your share of moments to escape from."

"Haven't we all?" she asked, letting out a heavy sigh.

Her question hung in the air between them, a rhetorical bridge neither fully wanted to cross.

EIGHTEEN

Now

The headlights of David's car cut through the darkness, illuminating the winding road ahead.

David's mind raced with thoughts of what could be lurking in the girl's past and what he was hiding himself. He glanced over at her—this young woman who had just saved him from potential scrutiny under the guise of being his daughter. She sat there, composed, gazing out into the rain-soaked darkness. He was grateful, yet the mystery of her presence gnawed at him. She had helped him, but deep down he felt as though it had not been an altruistic move: she had been helping herself just as much.

As the road stretched on, flanked by the impenetrable shadows of the woods, David felt the isolation of their journey weigh heavily upon him. The silence between them grew thicker, charged with unspoken questions. He wanted to ask her about her reasons for being out so late, about the secrets she might be keeping, but each time he nearly broached the subject, he hesitated. Revealing too much about his own curiosity could lead to questions he wasn't ready to answer. Instead, he focused on the road, the rhythmic swish of the windshield wipers providing a steady soundtrack to his racing thoughts.

He took a quick look at the clock, trying to calculate how long they had been driving, how many more bends they would have to navigate before the truck stop. Five minutes more? They were close.

He wouldn't leave her there. He would fill up, grab his coffee, maybe treat her to one too. He would enjoy a last few minutes of fake normalcy with the girl before getting back to the business of dealing with what he had done.

Maybe there, when she found the signal she needed to call whoever was going to pick her up and take her wherever was her final destination. Maybe there he would call Amanda.

She would be asleep, and she would be mad as hell, but he needed to hear her voice. He needed to be in touch with something in his life that could take away some of the desperation and deep, rotting guilt that he felt.

Guilt not only for what he had done that night, but guilt for his failings over their entire relationship.

That was too harsh. There had been a time when they had been happy. When he hadn't been a failure, too caught up in the job that slowly sucked the life out of him and sucked him out of his life. How long ago was that, though? Before they had Charlotte? Had his daughter only ever known the shitty sell out of a man that he was now?

181

People got what they deserved, and he deserved to pay for his actions.

He also deserved a strong coffee first.

And with that thought, it finally hit him.

"Shit!" he yelled the word like a primal impulse. "Shit, shit, shit," he repeated.

The girl jerked, startled, and immediately turned to the wing mirror.

There was nothing to see. David's trigger was internal. A realisation that he had made a fundamental mistake. One that could cost him dearly.

"Twenty-One," he said. "I'm sorry, but I'm going to have to ask for a favour."

"Favour?" she repeated, as though hearing the word for the first time.

"Yes," he said with unconcealed impatience.

A thought flickered into his mind about the Abraham Lincoln principle, and he pushed that thought away. He didn't need any reminders of earlier in the evening.

The girl ignored him and carried on staring blankly ahead.

"Look, I know I've probably pissed you off somehow," he said, recognising the passive aggressive response but not really understanding what had caused it. "I'm sorry. But I've helped you and now I need to ask you a favour in return."

She let out an irritated groan, the kind that his daughter might make when he asked her to bring the washing up out of her bedroom, and said, "What?"

David let out a breath before speaking. Frustration, tension, desperation. He had them all in spades. What he didn't have was the thing he needed the most.

"I don't have my debit card," David said. "I left it with my wife so she could buy damn pizza for her and my daughter."

"That's nice," the girl deadpanned. "I'm sure they take cash."

"Very nice," David sighed. "But I left my damn wallet in the bedroom. I don't have cash or a card. I can't get petrol without money, and if I can't get petrol, we are stuck out here."

His mind created a mental image of the scene, taking out his card, giving it to Amanda, not getting the hug in return. What did he ever get? Screwed over, that was what he got. That was all.

"*We* now, is it?" the girl said. "As far as I remember, you were telling me you wanted me gone. You want me to call Mummy or Daddy – neither of whom I can call, by the way, with them both being six feet under the ground."

"I thought we'd got past that," David said wearily. He snapped his mouth shut. That kind of response never worked for him, so he tried something else. "I'm sorry," David said, carefully. "Really. Shit. I'm sorry. I didn't know that, obviously. I'm so sorry," he repeated. "I never meant to make you feel like that. I don't want to get rid of you, and to clear up any kind of confusion between us here, I am not going to abandon you. I will make sure that you have someone to collect you. Shit, I'm sorry. But yes, I do think we are better off going our own ways. I do. But first, please. Can you help me out?"

"You're sorry, I get it," she said. "You didn't kill them. It's cool, really. You didn't know. I'm sorry for mentioning it, all right?"

The girl sighed, reached into her bag, and pulled out a small floral purse. Then, just before she opened it, she paused as though remembering something.

"I can't," she said. Her voice was suddenly small, almost silent.

"What?" David asked.

"I said I can't, okay?" She stuffed the purse back down deep into her bag, pushing it beneath whatever it was she had in there.

David watched while monitoring the road ahead, his mind spinning with confusion at her turnaround.

"I can pay you back, if that's the problem," he said. "If you don't have the money. I'm not asking you to actually pay for it, just, you know, use your card. I'm good for the cash. Look, I'm a guy who drives around in a company car in the middle of the night wearing a soaking tux. You can trust me."

He laughed, but the girl did not.

He looked at her again and saw only stone-faced composure.

"Twenty-One?" he asked. "Angeline?"

"I'm not Angeline, okay?" she snapped. "That's not my name. Don't call me that. Don't say that name ever again. I shouldn't have…I should never have said it. I shouldn't have…I…shit…"

"Hey," David said. "Hey. It's okay. Please. Calm down. Take a breath."

The girl was finally cracking.

"I don't want you to know my name. I don't want anyone to know my name, or that I was here, or…or…"

Her breath caught in her throat as the words sped from her mouth. A heat seemed to emanate from her body: frustration, emotion. David didn't know.

She pulled her hands up to her face, covering it from sight, dipping her eyes beneath her hood.

He was almost sure she was crying.

David let out a long, deep sigh.

"I'm sorry," he said.

Over and over, he had repeated apologies. When had anyone ever apologised to him? Not Amanda, not Charlotte, not Johnson, not Malcolm Mitchell. Not this girl. This stranger he was trying to help out. This weight around his neck.

"If I give you my card," she said, between sobs, "you'll know my name. They'll know my name.

They'll know who I am and where I am. They'll be able to…" She clapped her hand over her mouth and the sobbing gulps became heavier.

Whatever secret she was keeping, he couldn't let it jeopardise his ability to keep his own hidden. He needed to keep moving, and there was no way he could do that, not in this car without the girl's help.

As the fuel gauge neared empty and the silence between them stretched, David's frustration boiled over into decision. It was time to deal with what was sitting next to him.

He drove on. It wouldn't be much further. He knew the area well, these roads. It didn't take him long to think of an idea. That was his greatest skill, after all. It was what had made him the most valuable employee at Tursten Mitchell, no matter what Malcolm bloody Mitchell himself had thought. No matter whether Johnson was their blue-eyed man of the moment. He was the one who had the ideas. He had saved the company before, and now he was going to save himself.

The truck stop was close, but David had something else in mind. As he rounded the next bend, with a sudden twist of the wheel, David veered off the main road, not bothering to indicate.

"What are you doing?" the girl asked, her voice wavering.

He didn't look at her, but he could sense her agitation as she turned her head and then twisted her body, looking around to the sides of the car, out of the back window.

The narrow, winding track took them up an incline, climbing higher into the hills. The trees on each side of the road were closer here. The road was less well maintained, and the car skittered into potholes as they headed on.

"I said, 'what are you doing?'," the girl hissed like a cat that had been cornered.

David wanted to tell her that everything was going to be okay, that she was safe; no need to worry. He wanted to tell her that, but *he* needed to be safe. If she wasn't part of the solution, she was part of the problem, as the cliché went. Somehow, tonight, it felt chillingly true.

The car's headlights flickered across the wet foliage as they ascended, the storm enveloping them in an almost palpable shroud of isolation.

"There's a spot up here," David said, his voice tight with a mix of desperation and resolve. "A viewing area. We can stop there for a minute, sort things out."

The girl looked up, her eyes reflecting a mixture of surprise and what he read as fear.

"Sort. Things. Out." She repeated the words in a choppy punctuated string. "What do you mean, sort things out? Sort me out?"

She reached her hand towards the door, but David was faster. He clicked the central locking before she had time to pull the handle.

"Don't be stupid," he said, past caring about how he came across to her. "I need your help, okay? That's all. That's all this is." He looked at her and then focused on the road.

"We could have...I couldn't just...I..." She reached over towards him, her hand almost making contact with his arm, and then stopped as though frozen.

She sank back into her seat.

"I'm going to get what I wanted," she mumbled beneath her breath.

David looked over again.

The girl pulled her legs up to her chest and wrapped her arms around them, hugging herself tightly.

She's given up.

She was a scared girl all along.

The paternal flame flickered in David's stony heart, and he gently snuffed it out.

"It's okay," he said. "Everything is going to be okay."

He already knew, though, that each of those words was a lie.

Nothing was going to be anything near okay.

NINETEEN

Emma One Hour Ago

Being behind the wheel felt unfamiliar. Emma was a city girl; everything she needed was within walking distance. There was no need for her to run a car. Angeline had insisted that they should have one. *Just in case.* But in case of what, she didn't know.

The seat felt too close to the wheel, her legs cramped, her arms tentacle long. Her breaths came rapid and shallow, growing faster until Emma knew she was on the edge of claustrophobic panic.

She reached out and placed her hands on the rippled plastic of the steering wheel in the ten-to-two position in an attempt to ground herself. Driving had never felt natural to her, but now, tonight, with the destination she had in mind, it seemed completely alien.

It was time, though. She had to go. She had to follow Angeline. Walking through the city had done nothing to make her feel better.

She flicked a glance up at the mirror.

She couldn't bear to look at herself. Every time she did, she saw Angeline. She saw a worse version of her.

"Jeez. You look like shit," she muttered, turning her eyes away again.

I always look like shit.

This is me, now.

Even though her hands had only been resting on the cold plastic for a brief time, they were already clammy, and slipped as she adjusted her grip.

Get it together.

Again, she looked into the mirror, eyes on eyes, stern now, trying to force herself to gain composure.

"Get it together." The reflected lips moved in time with her own, but still Emma felt disconnected from the person she saw.

As she slid the key into the ignition, a flurry of vague thoughts flew across Emma's mind, like starlings startled by a sudden clap of thunder.

It's not going to start.

The battery will be flat.

Don't do this.

Don't do this.

Don't do this.

Emma continued to move her hand, metal gliding against metal. She turned the key.

A sudden blare of loud music erupted from the car's speakers, assaulting the silence with its unexpected ferocity. The force of the surprise jolted Emma back in her seat. Her hand withdrew sharply and clipped against the underside of the wheel, sending a judder of pain up her arm.

The shock of the noise, so stark against the backdrop of her brooding silence, momentarily scattered her dark thoughts like leaves caught in a gust of wind. Her heart pounded in her chest, an echo of the rapid beats blaring from the stereo, as she hurriedly fumbled to turn the volume down, her fingers trembling.

It was one of Angeline's CDs. Emma called them *archaic*, but Angeline preferred *retro*. The thing with Angeline was that she never tried to stand out, but something about her made her seem *otherly*. Somehow, they both were. Two peas in an impenetrable pod.

Still, Emma needed the music gone.

"Come the frick on!"

She rammed the volume control with a stiff finger.

For a moment, the world was reduced to the sharp pain in her hand, the throbbing in her chest, and the fading echoes of the music that had so abruptly invaded her space. There was an unsettling aura about the car's interior, as though she had not been invited to be there. It was still Angeline's, after all. As she turned the key all the way, the dashboard lit up with an array of lights that seemed to scrutinise her.

With a deep, shuddering breath, Emma steadied herself, her hand still hovering near the volume dial, as if afraid the car might betray her again. She glanced at the passenger seat, half-expecting, half-wishing to see Angeline there.

But the seat remained empty.

Emma took a moment to collect herself, the silence settling heavily around her like a thick fog. She couldn't shake the feeling of Angeline's absence, the space beside her a stark, unyielding reminder of the void that it had left.

"Why'd you have to go?" Emma whispered into the emptiness, her voice breaking with the weight of her loneliness.

The question was rhetorical; the answer lost, along with her sister. She reached over to the passenger seat, her hand brushing the fabric as if to reassure herself that she was indeed alone.

Her fingers itched for her phone, but she fought the urge.

If she didn't follow Angeline now, she never would.

The rain that had plagued her all evening showed no sign of letting up as Emma pulled out of the garage. Emma flicked up the stick on the right side of the steering wheel, and the amber ticking of her indicator mocked her.

Wipers, she muttered, correcting her mistake.

The windscreen was misty, even with the wipers in action, and she paused at the end of the short driveway to reach forward and wipe at it. Angeline kept an old festival T-shirt in the door pocket for such occasions. Once it had been Emma's. Now it probably belonged to Emma again.

Parklife, three years previously. A wild music festival where they had slept in a tent and partied far too hard. Emma was just old enough to drink, Angeline was just old enough to want to. This T-shirt had been covered in cider, mud and sweat, and - although her mind had tried to block it out - Emma remembered there was also a fair amount of vomit involved too. That was Angeline all over. Taking risks, pushing everything to excess.

If I hadn't made her have those drinks with me, she could have taken the car.

Whatever she was, she wasn't a drink-driver.

Emma pushed the thought out of her mind.

The jerky sensation of the car's movement added to Emma's unease. She gripped the steering wheel tightly, her palms still damp with sweat. The rhythmic ticking of the wipers seemed to taunt her, a reminder of her lack of experience behind the wheel.

Emma squinted through the streaked windscreen, straining to see the familiar landmarks of the city. She navigated the streets cautiously, sticking fastidiously to the speed limit. Driving wasn't something she could see herself getting used to. She was a passenger; always had been, always would be.

The streetlights blurred ahead of her. Emma forced herself to breathe, to focus on driving, despite the overwhelming feeling of being out of her element.

Two blocks down and she was back outside Urban Grind, closed now: dark and empty. Emma remembered the apple cake in her bag, but the thought of eating was the furthest thing from her mind. She knew Urban Grind was there, a waypoint in her journey onwards, but she didn't slow to look. Her visit earlier had been enough. She still had the taste of the coffee in her mouth: bittersweet.

Urban Grind was always their spot, where coffee turned into lunch. Sometimes it had turned into dinner, on the days they had nothing better to do than sit, watch the people on the street, and be together. Angeline's infectious laughter had a way of filling the space; Emma knew how much Vanessa loved her. In a way, throwing her out, sending her on her way was Nessa's way of showing she loved Emma, too.

If Nessa thought Emma would sit at home eating apple cake instead of carrying on her search for Angeline, she was wrong, wrong, wrong. Emma had committed to the path, and there was nothing that could stop her.

When she reached the park, Emma slowed. Its gates were locked in the night, now, its pathways hidden beneath the shroud of rain and darkness. Angeline was everywhere and nowhere.

She drove on, her grip on the steering wheel tightened as she drove over the bridge. She dared not look at the spot where the padlocks hung. She needed to focus on moving forward.

Had Angeline left the second engraved lock? And if so, when? Did she know she was leaving? It hardly seemed possible.

Shaking her head didn't dislodge the thought, but Emma tried. She wondered if there would ever come a day when her thoughts weren't consumed by her sister.

She pressed on, out beyond the edge of the city. Past the ring road, the apartments were replaced by squat houses, grass verges, the edge of the moorland drew near. The suburbs soon faded behind her. As she drove farther from the town, the hills in the distance grew closer, bleaker than ever beneath the storm laden night sky.

I shouldn't be out here alone, this late.
I shouldn't be here at all.

The moors, darker than the outskirts she had been driving through, loomed ahead. There was nothing out there. Nothing but the past, and that was a place she spent too much time visiting. Could she really follow the road she was on right to the one place she had never yet dared travel?

Against all odds, Emma's resolve started to waver.

She had set off with such certainty, such commitment to her path, but now, now she was so close, it seemed impossible to conclude her journey.

I should turn back.

Go home.

Eat the apple cake.

Tidy my damn room.

Live my stupid little life.

It was then that she saw her—a figure walking slowly by the side of the road, barely visible in the rain. A woman, alone, looking forlornly into the distance as if waiting for someone who would never come. Emma's first instinct was to drive past, to leave behind another reminder of her solitude. But something about the woman's posture, the way she seemed to carry her own world of pain, made Emma slow down.

Emma swallowed hard. This wasn't how the journey was supposed to be. She was a woman on a mission, and the mission was one that should be undertaken alone. Her mission was definitely not to pick up a passenger.

The words tattooed on her arm echoed in her ears, almost as though Angeline herself was speaking them.

`Everything happens for a reason.`

Emma slowed.

I was meant to be here tonight.

I was meant to pick up this woman.

I was meant to save her.

She engaged the indicator and applied pressure to the brake, coming to a stop beside the wet figure.

"Hi," she said, trying to sound as friendly and welcoming as possible. "Do you need a ride?"

The woman looked back at Emma with tear-filled eyes. Up close, Emma could tell that she had been crying for some time. She had a sudden urge to jump out of the car, run over and throw her arms around this stranger.

She did not know what was causing the woman's sadness, but she recognised the deep desolation.

Resisting the impulse, Emma called out again.

"Hey," Emma said. "You okay?"

The woman wiped her eyes before speaking.

"Yes, thanks," she replied. "Sort of."

Emma looked away to the road ahead, but left the window open, the car stopped.

What are you doing?

Her internal voice asked a question she couldn't answer.

Taking a deep breath, she looked out at the woman again.

"You need a ride?" Emma asked again, the words almost sticking in her throat.

The woman shook her head.

"I'm fine really," she said. But as her words stopped, they were replaced by deep sobs.

She hadn't driven past a building for a good mile. Whatever had led the woman to that place at that time of night, it couldn't have been anything good.

Emma pulled the car over towards the curb, looked into her rearview, and opened the passenger door.

"Come on," she said.

The woman hesitated, her figure wavering in the wash of the headlights against the stormy backdrop. The silent moors stretched ominously around them, the darkness swallowing everything except the small circle of light cast by the car. Emma could feel the weight of the desolate landscape press against her, a stark reminder of the loneliness that had brought her here, to this moment, on a road less travelled.

The woman's sobs cut through the patter of rain, a sharp reminder of human frailty in the night's vastness. Emma's heart thudded painfully against her chest, a mix of fear and resolve battling within her as she faced the stranger. Was this a rescue, or was she inviting more shadows into her already troubled life? The question hung in the air, unanswered, as the woman took a step towards the car, and climbed inside.

TWENTY

Now

As the car climbed higher, the city began to spread out beneath them in the distance, a sprawling canvas of twinkling lights that seemed detached from the reality of their cramped, tense existence inside the vehicle.

Finally, David pulled into the deserted viewing area. Gravel crunched under the tyres as he brought the car to a stop. They were high enough that the city below seemed like a different world, the buildings and streets reduced to miniature.

David killed the engine, and for a moment, they just sat there, the silence between them now a vast chasm, accentuated by the soft patter of rain on the roof. He turned to face her, trying to read her expression in the dim light.

"Look at it down there," he gestured towards the cityscape spread out below them. "From up here, it all seems so… insignificant. Like none of it matters. Like we never have to go back."

The girl was calm now. There was no fight left in her.

She followed his gaze, her eyes lingering on the distant lights. "It does feel that way, doesn't it?" Her voice was soft, reflective, a stark contrast to the tension that had filled the car just moments ago.

There was no trace of the fear he had perceived. Perhaps he had been wrong. Perhaps he had expected that a girl of her age in a stranger's car should be afraid to be driven off path. Perhaps he had wanted to scare her.

He gulped back the thought.

David's eyes lingered on the sleeping city below, its glow casting a serene veil over the chaos that seemed to swell within the confines of his car. The silence that had briefly felt like respite now turned heavy, an oppressive force that seemed to echo the pounding of his own heart. He turned to look at her again, her features faintly illuminated by the soft light from the dashboard. Her calm demeanour contrasted sharply with the storm of emotions raging inside him.

He had tried patience, he had tried understanding, but time and options were running out. The stark reality of their situation—the isolation, the dwindling fuel, the secrets swirling like the mist outside—began to gnaw at his resolve. His voice, when he finally broke the silence, carried an edge that hadn't been there before.

"I didn't mean to scare you, but I can't do this anymore," he started, his tone sharper than he intended. "We're stuck here. I've tried to be accommodating, to give you space, but that's over now. I need to use your card. I'm sorry that seems like such a huge deal to you but, that's the way it is."

"I can't," she said again. Her voice was flat now. "Do what you have to do. If you use my card, you might as well..." She made a throat slitting gesture with her finger.

David swallowed deeply.

"No one wants that. No one wants anything bad to happen here. But, listen. Listen carefully, because I'm not going to waste time repeating myself. If you don't start talking, if you don't tell me what's really going on, I'll leave you here. Right here, right now. I need you to trust me, and if you do, I will get you out of this, whatever's going on here."

He hoped he sounded genuine. All he needed was the card. He didn't need her. He didn't need the headache she had become.

The girl's eyes widened slightly, the first sign of real alarm crossing her face since they'd stopped.

"You can't be serious," she said, her voice a mixture of disbelief and fear. "You can't leave me here."

"I've never been more serious," David replied coldly. "I need to protect myself, and right now, I don't even know what I'm protecting *you* from. You have a means of getting us fuel and you're refusing to help. We could end up stranded. We are going to end up stranded unless you help me. Are you going to do anything to get us out of this? Are you going to just put your card on the table and damn well pay? Because if not, that makes you a liability."

He paused, letting the weight of his words sink in. The harshness in his own voice surprised him, but desperation had clawed its way to the surface, stripping away the last veneers of his composure.

"If you think I'm just going to sit here and risk everything for someone who won't even trust me with the truth, you're mistaken," he continued, his gaze steady and unyielding. "So, this is your last chance. Tell me. Just exactly what have you done?"

The tension between them crackled, nearly as palpable as the electricity in the storm-laden air outside. She looked away for a moment, out towards the city below, then back at him. Her jaw set, and when she spoke, her voice was low, tinged with a resignation that hadn't been there before.

"Okay," she said finally, a slight tremble in her words. "Okay, I'll tell you. But you have to promise me something first."

David's expression softened slightly, but he maintained his firm stance. "What is it?"

"You have to promise that no matter what I tell you, you won't leave me here alone."

It seemed such a simple, innocent request.

David swallowed and said, "Of course. I promise."

"Let's get out," she said. "It looks like the rain is finally stopping."

He eyed her for a moment. There was nowhere for her to run. Everywhere that wasn't illuminated by the headlights was pitch black. She wouldn't risk it.

"Okay," he said. "Don't do anything stupid."

She nodded, and David disengaged the lock.

The girl clicked open the car door and stepped out into the night.

The girl stood at the edge of the viewing area, her silhouette framed against the vast urban sprawl. David watched her for a moment, the tension between them now a tangible force that seemed to distort the air.

Slowly, he got out of the car and approached her, his footsteps soft on the wet gravel. He could see her shoulders rise and fall with deep, measured breaths.

"You were going to tell me something," he reminded her gently, his voice attempting to bridge the chasm of mistrust that had opened between them.

She turned to face him, her expression haunted, eyes reflecting the distant city glow.

"It's all gone wrong," she whispered, her voice barely audible over the soft whir of the distant city. "Everything... I didn't mean for any of this to happen. But I can't undo it now."

David's heart pounded with a mix of apprehension and sympathy.

"Tell me," he urged, stepping closer. "Maybe I can help. Maybe we can figure this out together."

She shook her head slowly, a sad smile flickering across her face as she looked back towards the city.

"It's too late for help. I've done things, David. Bad things… because I had to. Because I was scared. Because I was alone."

David's pulse raced. "What did you do?"

She didn't answer directly. Instead, she reached into her pocket slowly, deliberately. David tensed, expecting her to produce a weapon, but instead, her hand came out empty, clenched in a fist.

Before he could react, she swung her fist, striking him hard in the temple. The blow was unexpected and disorienting. David's head whipped to the side, stars bursting across his vision as pain radiated through his skull. He tried to grab her, to defend himself, but his reactions were too slow, his head spinning from the impact.

She struck him again, harder this time, directly in his windpipe. His senses blurred into confusion. As he slumped against the fence, dazed and struggling to maintain consciousness, she drew back again, landing another blow.

"I'm sorry, David," she whispered, as she pushed him with surprising strength. He tumbled down the slope back towards the car, landing heavily on the wet gravel. The ground was hard, the rocks jagged beneath him, as he tried to comprehend what was happening.

He tried to get up, but she had winded him badly. He opened his mouth to speak, but all he could do was gasp for breath.

She dragged him with a strength he had never imagined over to the open door of his car.

Was she going to pull him back inside? Drive them somewhere?

His fogged mind couldn't piece together what was happening.

The girl leaned over him, her silhouette framed against the dim light from the dashboard.

"I can't let you leave. You'd never understand. You'd never let it go," she said, her voice a mix of apology and resolve.

"You ask so many questions," she continued. "You want to know so much, but sometimes it's better to be two strangers in the night sharing a ride."

She sat him up, positioning his head, and slammed the door hard against it.

David tried to speak, to plead with her, but his words slurred. All that came was a howl of pain.

The girl broke out into a wide, out-of-place smile.

"That reminds me," she said, her eyes glowing with delirium. "You should have let me finish that joke earlier. The one about the hitchhiker."

David's expression didn't change. He tried to edge away, but he couldn't move. His limbs didn't respond to his brain's commands. He had a feeling that there was something terribly wrong.

The girl slammed the door again and stars burst inside David's broken head.

"He gets into the car and the driver says, 'You're brave, hitching a ride out here. Aren't you worried I might be a serial killer?'."

"And the passenger smiles and says, 'The chances of there being two serial killers in one car seems highly unlikely. Don't you think?'"

She glanced around quickly, then leaving him sitting in his rag doll position, she opened the rear door of the car. Reaching inside, she grabbed something from the back seat—a heavy flashlight. With a swift, regretful look, she raised it and brought it down hard against his head. The last thing David saw was a flash of light, not from the torch, but from the pain that exploded in his head.

David had one final thought before everything went dark.

I should call Amanda.

TWENTY-ONE

Now

She wasn't strong, not really. She'd never had the kind of job that demanded physical labour. She hadn't been interested in going to the gym. When Angeline had tried to talk her into attending self-defence classes, she had laughed it off, even after they had seen that woman in the park. That was until last year. Until Angeline…

Then, she had signed up, toned up, learned how an eight stone girl can down a six-foot man with a couple of punches in the right places. She would never be a victim like Angeline. She was a wasp now. She didn't look like much, but she knew how to sting.

Emma slipped her arms beneath the man's armpits, using her weight to pull him rather than carry him around to his parked car. The gravel worked like tiny wheels beneath him, helping her to drag him along.

He's not getting the deposit back on that suit.

Emma laughed at the random thought that had popped into her head.

What she should have been thinking about was how was she going to get back down to the road, how was she going to keep moving with no lift and no hope of getting one, where could she run to anyway? But none of those thoughts were funny, and before all that, there was work to be done.

His body was already cooling, out there in the early hour chill.

He wasn't a bad man.

I'm not sure he was a good man, either.

Although this wasn't the ending that David had planned, it seemed like the perfect place to Emma. Secluded, isolated, and lonely. She could happily spend the rest of her life somewhere like this.

There were no headlights to be seen on the road that they had driven up to reach the outlook. No one was coming.

Pulling David's keys from his pocket, she clicked the button to release the boot of his car. It began to rise immediately, with a slow, suspenseful creak.

She hitched her arms back under him and waited, calculating how she was going to hoist him up, tuck him in.

As the boot opened, though, Emma's jaw fell. Her arms went limp, letting David drop unceremoniously to the floor.

There was no way she could get the man into the trunk.

It was impossible.

He would never fit beside the body that was already there.

TWENTY-TWO

David One Hour Ago

David strode out of the Grand Hall, trying to look like a man who hadn't lost everything. He didn't stop to talk to any of his colleagues, and none of them tried to catch his attention. The black suits might as well have been funereal as celebratory. Tonight was the last night of David Burnham, senior manager. His head swirled with plans for the future. He had so much unused leave stockpiled that he could no doubt quit tomorrow; his three months' notice taken care of thanks to his fastidious work ethic. It would leave the company in the shit if he walked out, but they owed him, even before tonight they owed him.

He could retire. He didn't need the reference. Malcolm Mitchell could stuff it up his backside for all David cared. But, he knew, Amanda would see things differently.

First, she would be livid that he had made such a major decision about his own life without consulting her. Sure, it was fine for her, when she took maternity leave with Charlotte and decided she enjoyed staying at home more than she enjoyed working. Not staying at home to be a mother, that was never part of her plan; she wanted to stay at home for the social perks of the position. Sitting around in restaurants with the other mothers was far more appealing to her than working for a living.

Did David have a say in that?

Amanda hadn't even discussed it.

Then, of course, she would worry about where the money was coming from if he left Tursten Mitchell. They had savings, but savings were to be saved, according to Amanda. They could fester in the bank while David festered in his job.

If she needed to spend them, though, it was different. Holidays, clothes, a little treat every now and again, which was always more like now, now, now; Amanda ruled from the top.

It was no wonder that Michael knew so much about Amanda. She was the personality in their relationship. He was an extension of her, and until tonight, he had been comfortable in the role. He treated his position as husband with the same reverence as he had his position in the company. He put in maximum effort for little reward.

What did anyone really know about him? What did he even know about himself anymore?

The disaster of the night was what he needed. He could take a gap year. Could you still call it that if you were a forty-five-year-old man with a demeaning wife and a demanding kid?

He could travel. Peru. China. He had never even made it as far as Edinburgh. Now was his chance.

All of these thoughts were attempts to make light of the worst of nights. If he did nothing, carried on as normal, Michael had won; there was no way David was going to let that happen.

David was going to do something spectacular.

He was going to change his life, and he was going to do it for himself.

As he stepped outside, the night air hit David with an icy slap. The rain maintained a relentless downpour that seemed to mock David's turmoil. Despite his ticking thoughts, the ire continued to boil in his veins. The droplets splashing against his face did little to cool him down.

David made a beeline for his car, his mind a maelstrom of anger, frustration, and the gnawing suspicion Michael had planted chewing at the edges of his consciousness. The weight of the evening – Michael's victory, the whispered insinuations about Amanda – bore down on him as he crunched down the drive to the car park. How different it felt, walking back alone.

Pausing beside his car, David fumbled for his phone, the screen a blur through the rain-slicked veil covering his eyes. He typed a message, a simple *Are you awake?* to Amanda. His thumb hovered over the send button, a hesitation born of doubt and the fear of what her answer, or lack thereof, might signify. With a weary sigh, he pressed **send**; the message disappeared into the ether, a digital missive carrying a fragment of his disappointment with it.

Before he could pocket the phone, a flicker of light caught his eye. A figure of a man.

It couldn't be.

Not one last opportunity to torment him?

But it was.

Michael, standing a few cars away, cigarette in hand, an aura of superiority emanating from him even in the dim glow of the car park lights. Here, away from the polite etiquette of Henderson House and company policy, David could speak his mind.

That split second, the decision whether to step into his car and leave or to give Michael what was coming to him, was a threshold between past and future.

He could walk away.

He could choose to let it go.

He didn't.

"Burny," Michael called over, and started to move in his direction.

David stood in place; confrontation, it seemed, was inevitable.

As he approached, Michael took another drag, the tip of the cigarette glowing bright against the night.

"Not worth grabbing the umbrella just for a fag," he said with a nonchalant shrug, waving the cigarette like a sparkler.

"You're staying then? Going back in?" David asked, nodding toward the venue. He didn't care.

The sophisticated façade of the evening had crumbled away, leaving behind the raw, unvarnished truth of their rivalry, exposed under the harsh, unyielding rain.

"There are only hangers on and drunks in there," Michael said, his voice carrying a note of disdain that grated on David's already frayed nerves. "The fun part is over."

He pulled the trophy out from under his jacket where he had been shielding it from the weather. He was carrying it around with him as though he couldn't possibly put it down. David was simultaneously disgusted and enthralled.

Michael slipped the award back into its safe place, and added, "But there's still plenty of free champagne, and who doesn't love that?"

David eyed him steadily.

"Me," he said. "I haven't touched a drop."

His voice lacked any sense of emotion. David was controlled; he knew he had to be.

Michael stood motionless, watching his colleague for a moment before speaking.

"Do you know what, mate? Sometimes I think you might be terribly dull."

Was he? Probably.

He'd put his life's efforts into his job. He'd raised his small yet perfect-to-him family with a wife he loved. He didn't drink, didn't smoke. The only drug he had ever touched was caffeine, but God did he love it.

David smiled, and despite his inner distress, he meant it.

"I'd rather have my life than yours," he said.

"But I have this," Michael said, pulling out the trophy again and waving it mockingly towards David. "And I've had other things of yours, too. I'm sure you must know that."

David swallowed hard.

"You do, don't you?" Michael continued, moving towards him. "You didn't want to admit to yourself that the award was going to be mine…and you don't want to admit that Amanda is mine, too. Of course, I was going to win. I knew weeks ago. You're too bloody stupid to figure anything out, Burny mate."

Michael's words were a drunk, sprawling drawl, slurred together through his thick smile.

David stood in stunned silence, but it wasn't the confirmation of the relationship that stung the sharpest. The confirmation that his employer had screwed him over hurt more than anything Amanda could have done.

"You knew? About the award?" David asked eventually, his voice so quiet it was almost inaudible.

"Me?" Michael's smile broadened. "Everyone in the company knew, David. I thought *you* knew." He took a drag on his cigarette and blew a long stream of white smoke from his nose. "Jeez, man. How did you not?" Seeing the defeated look on

David's face seemed to mellow him slightly. "Listen, I would have told you if I knew you were going to—"

"What?" David was louder, now. "If I was what?"

"If you were going to act like a teenager about it, that's what." Michael flicked the still glowing butt of his cigarette into the darkness of the night.

David's eyes widened, and he drew himself up into a full-on standing position.

"*Teenager*? I can't believe what I'm hearing. Teenager? Is that…?"

The rain had soaked through David's hair and was running in rivulets down his face. He slicked it back with his fingers, both hands at once. It was driven by a need to do something, to move, to have something to focus on other than what the bastard next to his car was saying.

Amanda.

He couldn't deal with her betrayal yet.

He didn't want to give Michael the satisfaction of even acknowledging that truth. Instead, he had to focus on the glass trophy in front of him and the arsehole that was holding it.

Michael was still talking.

"I know I haven't been with TM as long as you have, Burny, but look at what I've achieved."

"Three years," David said, the pitch in his voice escalating. "Three. I've been with Tursten Mitchell…" He emphasised the full name rather than following Michael in using the initials. "…for eleven bloody years. Over a decade."

"So, you didn't win last time either?" Michael said, as if it meant something.

"Do you know why? Because I'd been at the company for a year, that's why. Because you don't just come along and…and…you don't just…"

It was too much. The emotion was bubbling in his chest, and it was about to come to the boil. There was no way David could let himself cry in front of Michael, but he needed to do something. He had to let out the steam that was building.

"There's always next time," Michael said, with another sickly smile.

He tucked the trophy beneath his arm and took a step towards David. His hand reached forward; it was the final straw.

Without fully realising what he was doing, David lashed out, his hand connecting with Michael's smug face. The impact sent the trophy clattering to the wet gravel, a crunching echo in the quiet night. Michael stumbled back, shock and anger flashing across his features.

For a moment, the world seemed to pause, the rain the only sound in the sudden silence. David stood, chest heaving, staring at Michael with a mix of satisfaction and horror at his own actions. The line had been crossed; the unspoken rules of their engagement shattered.

"What…" Michael began to speak, but David was on him again.

He swung his fist, putting the full force of his weight and the night he had just endured into the blow.

The younger man dropped to the floor, his hand reaching up to the site of the impact, as though he couldn't believe what was happening.

"David," Michael said, trying to pull himself up.

But David aimed a kick at his colleague's chest, forcing him back down.

As he fell for the second time, a guttural, gurgling cry escaped from his lips.

And then, he was silent.

David was already in motion, his foot raised above Michael's chest, when he realised that something was very wrong.

Michael was limp, unmoving.

David paused, foot still mid-air, and looked down.

"Michael?" He spoke the word cautiously, as if he was afraid that he was about to be the victim of yet another callous prank.

When Michael failed to respond, David brought his foot back towards himself, then quickly crouched behind his colleague.

"Michael," he repeated, with urgency.

But Michael was silent.

Rain fell into his open eyes and rivered away down his face.

"Michael?" David whispered the word into the man's ear, as though trying to speak to his soul.

There was no soul to hear him.

As David reached to put his hand on Michael's neck to feel his pulse, he saw the pool of blood that was barely visible from his standing position but now, down here, was hard to miss, even in the near darkness.

By his side, Michael's award lay, the tip covered in dark, sticky blood from where it had sliced Michael's jugular.

Perhaps banging his head had been a blessing. Perhaps he had felt nothing other than the dull thud that knocked him out.

"Oh shit," David said. "Shit, shit, shit."

Despite the severity of his situation, David kept his voice quiet, repeating the words in a mutter.

He lifted his head to look around the carpark.

There was no one around.

Just the two of them.

One alive, one dead.

TWENTY-THREE

Emma One Hour Ago

The rain pattered rhythmically against the car as Emma drove on, the silence in the vehicle thick with unspoken thoughts. If everything happened for a reason, Emma was meant to meet this woman. She just didn't know why.

Eleven at night, out of town, standing by the roadside could surely only end in trouble.

"Bad night?" Emma asked.

The woman let out a soft chuckle. "Yeah, well, I guess you could say so. Had a bit of a row with my roommate—well, ex-roommate now. Things got pretty heated, and I just had to get out of there."

Emma nodded, understanding the need for escape all too well. "That bad, huh?"

"You could say that. She's convinced I stole something from her, something valuable. Accusations flew, threats followed, and I just... I couldn't stay there. Not with the air so thick you could cut it with a knife." The woman's voice was tinged with a weariness that spoke of deeper hurts than just a simple argument; a deeper relationship than two roommates.

"So, you walked out? Just like that?" Emma asked, glancing briefly at the young woman's face lit by the dash display.

"Yeah. Grabbed my bag and left. Didn't even know where I was going until I ended up on the road. Then I got the idea in my head. There's a place I used to go with my mum, only another mile or so ahead." She shrugged, a gesture meant to seem carefree but betrayed by the tension in her shoulders.

Emma's grip on the steering wheel tightened slightly. "Heading to the hills at this time of night because of a fight? That's pretty drastic."

The woman sighed, her breath fogging up the window beside her as she watched the rain streak down its surface. "It sounds crazy, I know. But it's not just about the fight. It's everything, you know? This was just the last straw. I've been feeling trapped, like I'm stuck in a loop of bad days. I thought maybe if I got away for a bit, saw something new, it might help me figure things out."

"Or at least give you a break from the drama," Emma added softly, understanding the need to flee from one's own life all too well.

"Exactly. Yeah. I guess I just wanted to talk to my mum. The place I'm headed, it's only a couple of miles from home. Mum always said it had the best view of the stars. Figured if there's any place to clear my head, it'd be there. Seems a lot further in the dark, though."

The woman gave a tight-lipped smile that reminded Emma so much of her own fake bravery.

"It sounds like a good place to start," Emma responded, trying to sound supportive. "I'm happy to give you a lift, but…do you really think you should be out there on your own at this time of night? I know things are bad for you right now, but…"

Emma paused. Tears were flooding down the woman's face.

"I'm glad I found you," Emma said. "I can wait a while and bring you back down to town again. I kind of understand what you're going through."

The woman turned to look at her, a wisp of a smile crossing her features. "Thanks," she said. "Thanks for not driving past. For listening. It feels good to talk to someone who gets it. I think that's what I needed really: someone to talk to. When I get to the hill, I'll talk to my mum. Even though I know she can't hear me."

"Maybe she can," Emma said, thinking of all the calls she still made to Angeline.

The woman laughed, sucking the warmth out of their shared space.

"She's been dead for six years, love. I don't think she'll be hearing much of anything these days."

Something about the woman's words jabbed into Emma like a knife. Here she was, trying to be helpful, being a decent human, nice, friendly, and this woman…

"You still talk to her, though?" Emma asked, trying to turn the conversation back towards the positive.

"I know I'm only talking to myself. It's a way of getting all the shit out of my brain. Everything I'm going through at home. I pretend I'm telling Mum, but…love, she is dead, and the dead are not around to hear us."

Emma swallowed hard and looked dead ahead, watching the lines of rain in the beam of Angeline's headlights.

"If there was any such thing as ghosts, believe me, my mum would have been back here, haunting me every day. She would never let me have a moment's rest." The woman laughed again, the sound caustic against Emma's ears.

"I'm not saying that I believe in *ghosts*," Emma said with more bitterness than she had planned. "But I lost my sister. I lost my sister and I like to think she is still with me."

"Sure," the woman said unconvincingly. "In our memories, they are with us."

"More than that," Emma whispered.

She couldn't let it go. If this was the hill she was going to die on, so be it, but she would not let this stranger devalue her feelings. She was doing the woman a favour, and in return, the woman was trashing her beliefs.

Tonight was not the night.

Emma began to feel a dull throb in her temples as her tension rose. The medication she had taken earlier had done its job to fight off the migraine, but now, with the stressor sitting beside her, she could sense another storm brewing.

Despite what she felt, she had to change the direction of the conversation. There was no point trying to share the memories of their loved ones when all it was doing was causing pain, emotional and physical.

Emma took a deep breath and tried something different.

"I guess it's lucky I was coming past," Emma said, her voice tinged with a mixture of concern and a caution born of her own deep-seated fears. "Out there on your own. Some people might think it was dangerous. You know…"

"Dangerous?" The woman's laughter sliced through the tension that Emma's words had woven, sharp and dismissive.

Emma shot a look in her direction, her eyes narrowing, the shadows in the car making her expression seem even more severe.

"It's late. You were out in the dark. You're…" Emma hesitated, the final word hanging between them like a verdict waiting to be pronounced. "You're vulnerable."

"Okay, okay," the woman laughed again, the sound grating on Emma's already frayed nerves. "I'm sorry, but I don't think you know me. Don't think because I was out there, alone, that I'm weak. Don't assume that because I accepted a lift, I'm some kind of victim-in-waiting."

Her defiance was palpable, a challenge thrown into the night air between them.

They had started out on the wrong foot, and now it appeared they were heading down the wrong road head to head.

Emma swallowed, the breath catching in her throat, the taste of her own mounting frustration bitter on her tongue.

"Look, this isn't really helping me," the woman said. "Why don't you just pull over and let me out? I'll make my own way. I'll be just fine."

The word *just* stretched out in a long, mocking whine, slicing through Emma's patience like a knife.

"And what? Leave you by the side of the road in the middle of nowhere?" Emma shook her head, the motion so vehement her earring slapped against her cheek, a stinging reminder of the reality they both faced.

"Yes, thanks," the woman said firmly, leaving no room for discussion. "Stop. Let me out."

"Did you not hear that a woman was killed…up here…" Emma's hand waved vaguely towards the road ahead, her voice pitching higher, a note of desperation creeping in. She struggled to maintain control, to keep the panic at bay. "It was a year ago."

"Yes, terrible," the woman said dismissively. The only emotion in her tone was anger. "I can look after myself. We are literally two miles out of town. I can manage to get that far, thank you very much," she said. "Now stop and let me the hell out."

The woman reached over and tugged on Emma's arm.

"What the hell?" Emma hissed. "Don't!"

The car's engine hummed quietly as tension crackled in the confined space, a stark contrast to the dark, silent world outside. Emma's hands were clenched tightly around the steering wheel, her knuckles white with the effort of keeping the vehicle steady despite the storm brewing inside her.

"You don't get it, do you?" Emma's voice was tight, each word measured, but laden with an unspoken weight.

The woman beside her, the woman whose name she didn't even know, exuded a confidence that grated on Emma's already frayed nerves.

"I get that I don't want to be in this car anymore," the woman retorted, her tone heavy with irritation. "I told you; I can take care of myself. I only took the lift because of the damn rain."

The insistence, that stubborn belief in her own invulnerability, stung Emma. It was like listening to Angeline all over again, always so sure, always so fearless—until fear was all they had left.

With a sigh that felt like it carried the weight of the world, Emma pulled the car over into a shallow layby, the tires crunching on the broken branches at the side of the road. The abrupt stop sent a silence sprawling through the car, thick and suffocating.

"Why do you care anyway?" The woman's voice cut through the quiet, less defiant and more curious now that the car was motionless.

Emma turned to her, the pain and frustration that had been building up over the course of the night spilling over.

"Because today marks a year since my sister, Angeline, was killed. She thought she could handle everything on her own, too."

The woman's face softened, her previous defiance melting away in the face of Emma's raw grief.

"I… I didn't know. I'm sorry. The woman?"

"She was my sister," Emma hissed. "She was my sister, and someone murdered her."

The woman's discomfort was palpable. There were no words to respond adequately to what the driver was saying.

She paused, her hand on the door handle, turning back with a look that mingled sympathy with impatience.

"I'm sorry about your sister. But that doesn't change *my* situation. I still need to go. I can't…"

Emma couldn't find any more words to keep the woman safely in her car.

The passenger opened the door, and the cold air rushed in, carrying with it the scent of rain and earth. The vehicle's interior light flickered on. The woman, without another word, grabbed her bag and stepped into the night.

"Wait!" Emma's voice cracked.

She opened her own door and followed, her breath visible in the air as she spoke.

She watched, heart sinking, as the woman began to walk away, her steps quick and decisive.

There was nowhere to go. They were two miles out of Maplewood; in the direction the woman was walking, there was nothing but desolate moorland, danger, darkness. Sitting under the stars talking to a dead mother that she didn't believe could hear suddenly seemed to Emma like a death wish.

Panic and an unexpected surge of fear for the woman's safety drove Emma onwards. She stood at the edge of the road, raindrops pelting her face as she called out, "Please, don't go! I'm sorry—I just…It's not safe. Please."

Her words trailed off into the sound of the storm.

The woman, propelled by a seemingly desperate need for distance, broke into a run. Her figure, illuminated intermittently by the car's headlights, seemed ghostly, almost ethereal against the dark backdrop of the forest.

Emma, unable to let go, chased after her.

"Stop, please!" she cried out, her voice drowned by the roar of the wind.

The ground beneath her feet was slick with rain, the moonless night disorienting.

Up ahead, the woman's silhouette stumbled—the terrain, uneven and treacherous in the darkness, had betrayed her. Emma watched in horror as the woman's foot caught in a hidden dip in the ground, her body pitching forward uncontrollably.

There was a terrifying moment of clarity as Emma saw the woman's head smash against a jutting rock. The sound of the impact—a dull, sickening thud—echoed through the stormy night, freezing Emma in her tracks.

She stood stock still for a moment, shock pinning her to the spot. Finally, she forced herself to move. She looked down at the shape of the woman.

The stranger's eyes were open, staring blankly at the sky, the life already fading from them.

"Hey," Emma said. "Can you hear me?"

The woman seemed to look through Emma. She moved her lips, but no sound came out.

Tears mixed with the rain on Emma's face as she realised the finality of what had occurred. A tragic accident—a life lost in a moment of panicked flight. Emma sat back on her heels, the rain soaking through her clothing, chilling her to the core as she stared at the still form before her.

"I didn't mean for this... I just wanted to talk," Emma whispered into the void, her voice lost in the storm.

She covered her face with her hands, sobbing, overwhelmed by a profound sense of guilt and shock. The night, once merely dark and unsettling, had turned into a tableau of tragedy and irreversible consequences.

Emma sat on the wet ground by the roadside, staring at the body. The surrounding woods seemed to close in, the shadows of the trees casting long, accusing fingers. The woman's body lay as a stark testament to the fragility of life and the devastating impact of fear-driven decisions.

The woman's dead eyes seemed to stare straight at Emma, judging her, condemning her.

It was an accident, but it was Emma's fault.

She knew it.

As the storm continued unabated, Emma realised she needed to decide—leave and seek help, or stay and face the consequences of what had happened. Or...was there another option?

She switched on her phone, clicked on the flashlight, and shone it around her. More than anything else, she was looking for a sign. Something. Anything.

Behind her, the headlights of Angeline's car illuminated both Emma and the trouble she had caused. If she didn't make a decision, it would be made for her.

Her mind was a maelstrom of thoughts. Nothing made sense.

Emma felt an overwhelming urge to reach out, close the woman's eyes, and let her sleep in peace, but instead, she stood and stepped away.

She scanned the area with her torch, still hoping that a plan would come to mind.

There has to be a way out of this.

If there was, she couldn't see it by the dull, useless light of her phone and the beams of the headlights of the car she so desperately wanted to get back into.

But getting into the car had been a mistake.

Driving, coming out here. She had followed Angeline's journey, and it had ended in death.

Again, death.

The journey was over. This was the end.

The car.

I have to ditch the car.

The thought came to Emma with such bold certainty.

Leave the woman, ditch the car.

It's the only way.

She could turn around, head home. She could drive on, over the hills, into the next town, but then what? Where could she possibly go now?

It was an accident, but she was to blame.

She was a murderer.

She knew it.

Emma looked down at the woman one final time.

"I'm sorry," she said, choking back a sob. "I'm so sorry."

Stepping away from the body, Emma got back into the driver's seat. She needed the car out of sight. There would be tracks, it would be traced. It would not take long.

The more she tried to make a rational plan, the more impossible it seemed.

Emma's hands trembled as she drove on, leaving the woman exposed in the lay-by. The next person to stop would find her, but travellers were few on the moor at night.

Her hands were goosebump dimpled, damp and slippery. All she wanted was to stop the car.

She swerved off the road, through a gap in the trees, and looked for a place to leave her past behind.

The car gone, Emma walked. The ground underfoot was a tapestry of wet heath and hidden dips, each step an unpredictable dance with danger. The wind whipped around her, echoing her own chaotic thoughts. She had left the car—her last link to the semblance of safety—behind, propelled by a wild, desperate hope.

She stumbled forward, her breaths coming in ragged gasps, each one a white puff against the chilly night air. The moor stretched out endlessly before her, a vast expanse of nothingness. Yet, somewhere within her, a flicker of hope stirred— a hope so fragile and irrational, it frightened her. It whispered of rescue, of salvation, of being found and saved from the consuming emptiness that threatened to swallow her whole.

"Someone will come," she murmured to herself, her voice barely audible above the storm. The words felt foolish even as they left her lips, but she clung to them, needing to believe in their possibility. It was a mantra, repeated over and over, pushing her legs to move when all she wanted was to collapse into the wet undergrowth and let the night take her.

The reality of her situation was stark; she was lost, both physically and metaphorically, on a moor that offered no guidance, no path to salvation. The darkness seemed to press in from all sides, tangible and suffocating, yet she continued to move forward, driven by the need to escape her past and the ghost of her sister that lingered in every shadow.

Her phone, secured in her pocket, was her only lifeline to the world she had left behind, and there was no signal out here. Even if there had been, there was no one left to call. There had to be someone else, someone coming for her—not her calling out to them. That would mean something, wouldn't it? That she mattered, that her life wasn't just a series of missteps and mishaps?

As she had the thought, a light appeared suddenly—a distant, bobbing lantern light that seemed too serendipitous to be real. Emma's heart leapt. Was this it? The rescue she had conjured from her desperate thoughts? She quickened her pace, her eyes fixed on the light, her mind racing with possibilities. But as she drew closer, the light flickered and died, snuffed out by the wind, leaving her in darkness once again.

Disheartened yet undeterred, Emma pressed on. The irrational hope that had sparked her journey did not wane. It was a beacon, albeit one of her own making, guiding her through the night.

Finally, exhausted and nearly delirious, Emma made her way back to the road and walked. She pressed onwards, further onto the moors, head bowed against the storm, waiting for a sign, any sign, that her hope was not in vain. That somewhere, somehow, someone was searching for her, ready to pull her from the precipice on which she teetered.

The night offered no answers, only the relentless sound of the storm, as merciless and unyielding as fate. Emma's shoulders sagged, the weight of her isolation settling in like a cold shroud. Yet, she whispered into the dark, one last time, "Please, find me." Her words were a plea to the void, to the universe, to anyone who might be listening, a final, desperate hope she would not be left to face the dawn alone.

And then, the headlights appeared.

TWENTY-FOUR

Now

Silence enveloped the overlook, dense and suffocating, as Emma stood rooted to the spot. Her gaze was locked on David's body, sprawled ungracefully beside the car. She couldn't bring herself to look at the stranger in the trunk; the other passenger who had travelled with them all along.

The image was already seared into her mind. The pale man in the sharp suit: almost a match for David's own outfit. A colleague, for sure. Not a friend, though, it seemed.

It was too much for her adrenaline-addled brain to compute. It explained so much, but left so many more questions open, never to be answered.

For now, all she could do was speculate, and she had little time for that. The pieces were starting to fit together, though. The man she had only known for this brief time hadn't seemed the sort to even raise his voice until the point that his back was against the wall. If she could have used her card, if she hadn't been so desperate to hide her own identity, to protect herself, she might never have known about the other passenger.

Or she might have ended up laying next to him anyway.

A body. Jeez, David. What happened tonight?

The dead man on the ground could never give her any answers.

"David," she said, crouching to sit beside him. "I…" She paused. There was no point asking a corpse anything. "Shit, man. Shit. Look…I didn't mean for this to happen. You have to understand. It was you or me. Maybe that's how it was for you and…"

She nodded up towards the trunk.

Despite his inability to respond, a series of trill pings burst from David's pocket, making Emma jolt away. Her hand grazed against the gravel and she drew it in towards herself, wincing in pain.

His phone. He finally had a signal.

Someone out there is going to miss David.

A warm tear trickled down Emma's face, and she wiped it away.

She had set out that night to follow Angeline's path; all she had done was leave paths for other people to follow.

Emma's blood ran as cold as the early morning air as she leant towards David and slipped her hand into his pocket. No caution now, not like earlier. Her fingerprints were all over the car already. Her heart was too heavy to cover up what she had done.

David's phone was a generic slab, locked of course, but on the screen was a list of notifications. One text message. Two missed calls from Amanda. One more message.

Taking a breath, Emma let her finger rest on the phone screen. There was no way she could open the device; it was password locked, none of the facial recognition that her own phone offered. The thought sent another shudder through Emma; would she really have held the handset up to the dead man's face?

She could see the messages on the lock screen preview.

The first.

Yes.

One word, no context. It meant nothing to the girl.

The second.

I know you must be disappointed not to have won the stupid award, but that's no reason to ignore my calls. Lottie is worried about you. I'm going to bed. Sleep on the sofa.

Emma looked up at the man's face. Slumped in his suit, even with the blood congealing on his face and the way his tongue lolled out of his mouth, he looked at peace. Wasn't he looking for a way out of his unsatisfactory little life? From what little Emma had gleaned about Amanda, she didn't think that the widow was the type to feel the loss in the same way she had.

Lottie, though? Charlotte.

Emma swallowed hard.

She was trying to protect herself, but what had she done?

The girl was almost her age. The age Angeline would have been now.

What would Angeline have thought of the chaos and death, death, death?

If everything happened for a reason, couldn't that reason sometimes be that people were capable of making terrible mistakes?

Emma's eyes prickled with tears as she slid the phone back into the David's pocket.

The ground was rough, and Emma couldn't help but feel that she should move the man who had brought her there; make him more comfortable. It was a ridiculous, instinctive response. She had never been responsible for a dead body before, and now here she was, for the second time in the same night.

Beside David, Emma's movements were shaky and uncertain. She touched his cheek, startling back at the coldness of his skin. A shudder ripped through Emma, a visceral reaction not to the chill in the air but to the finality of his stillness.

She hadn't touched the woman, thinking back then that she should be careful, not leave a trace of herself. The woman's death had been an accident, but she knew it was her fault. She knew she would pay for it anyway. David's death was unquestionably all on her. Once she had started, she couldn't stop. An interminable force had driven her.

Everything happens for a reason, and the reason had been Emma.

"It wasn't supposed to end like this," she murmured to the quiet, her voice a fragile thread of sound in the vast stillness. The words fell flat, swallowed by the enormity of her solitude.

She knew that this time she was talking to herself. There was no attempt to commute with the dead, only her useless words spoken into the empty night.

Emma wrapped her arms tightly around her body, a meagre shield against the wave of despair threatening to overwhelm her. Here she was, utterly alone.

Her hands, cold and trembling, fumbled through her pockets until they closed around her phone. David had finally, too late, managed to receive messages. Perhaps she could get a connection, too. Emma watched as the screen flickered, showing a few bars of signal—enough to make a call.

She paused, her breath visible in the chilly air, the decision weighing heavily on her. There was only one number she ever found herself dialling, one voice she needed to hear, even if it was only in her head. As the phone rang, unanswered, Emma imagined her sister, Angeline, picking up, her voice soft and forgiving.

There was no answerphone message for her to talk to, no trace of her sister's voice. The phone rang on into endless emptiness, as it always had every time she had called over the past year.

From those first hours when Emma found her way home without her sister, and her sister never found her way home at all. From Emma falling asleep drunk and dizzy, but wanting to hear her sister's voice, waking up alone in the flat, calling frantically over and over.

They were always together; they went out together; they came home together. Always safe. Then that night, Angeline wanted to stay out. One more drink. Half an hour. Stay, Emma. Stay.

But she had not. There was work in the morning; she had to sleep off the vodka - so Angeline stayed alone.

Emma never understood why and knew she never would.

Perhaps not everything happened for a reason. Sometimes the world was just a shitty place and bad things happened to the best people.

"Angeline," Emma whispered into the phone, her voice breaking as she sank to her knees on the cold ground. "I'm so sorry. It's all my fault. I let you down that night… let you drink too much… let you walk alone. I should have been there. I should have protected you."

Tears streamed down her cheeks, her words a torrent of grief and guilt. "If I'd been with you when you walked over the bridge…If I'd been with you, you would never have taken that lift." Emma's voice was broken by sobs. "I just wanted to understand what you went through, to feel what you felt in your last moments. I thought… I thought if I could just experience it, maybe I could understand. But it was a mistake, Angeline. This was all a terrible mistake. Everything's gone wrong and I have no way of putting it right again."

The line remained silent, her own heaving cries filling the void where she wished her sister was.

"I don't know what to do now. I'm lost, Angeline. I'm so lost without you."

She clutched the phone to her chest; the device pressed against her heart as if it could bridge the gap between her and her sister's memory.

"I love you," she whispered. "I'm so sorry."

Memories of the night Angeline died haunted her, shadows flitting through her mind, urging her towards a decision. Emma had played those scenes over in her head, countless times, each replay a stab of guilt: the laughter at the bar, the last hug goodbye, the horror of the phone call the next morning. She had replayed her sister's last night from imagined moments of fear, her desperate escape attempts, to her tragic, untimely end. Emma had been trying to piece together a puzzle that only led to more despair.

"Goodbye, Angeline." Emma's voice broke as she spoke the last words.

With a deep, shuddering breath, Emma ended the call and stared out across the overlook.

She knew what she had to do next.

Standing up, her resolve slowly knitting together the fragments of her shattered self, Emma dialled another number. This time, the line connected immediately.

"999, what's your emergency?" came the dispatcher's voice, clear and calm.

"Police. I need to report two bodies," Emma said, her voice steadier than she felt. She stumbled slightly as she corrected herself. "Three bodies. There's been a terrible accident."

She gave them the location, her words precise, the finality in her voice mirroring the firmness of her decision. After providing all the details, she hung up, and walked back over to where she had left David propped against the car.

"I'll never know your story," she said, tilting her head, looking down at the man's corpse, "but I know one thing: Everything happens for a reason."

Emma tried to believe the line. She bent to leave her phone beside David on the ground. Then she stepped away and began to walk upwards, to the topmost part of the overlook.

Emma stood alone at the edge of the steep drop, the chilly dawn air brushing against her face like a whisper. Below, the city was sleeping, unaware of the turmoil that had unfolded through the night. She had made her call, her voice steady over the line as she reported what needed to be said, leaving nothing out. The phone lay beside David, a silent testament to her final confession.

As she looked out over the horizon, the stars looked brighter than she had ever seen them before. The storm had given way to a clear velvet night, the stars diamonds, stitched into its fabric. It was beautiful and serene, a stark contrast to the chaos within her. The world was quiet, the earlier tumult of the storm forgotten, as if the earth itself had exhaled and settled into a peaceful stillness. Emma felt the weight of her actions, the gravity of her choices pressing down on her with unbearable heaviness.

She took a deep breath, the air filling her lungs with a cold bite. She was a tumult of emotions—guilt, grief, resolution, and an indescribable weariness. It had all started with a desire to understand her sister's last moments, to walk the path Angeline had walked, to punish herself for her perceived failings. But the journey had led her here, to a moment of profound solitude and decision.

Emma stepped forward, her boots crunching softly. Each step was deliberate, a slow march towards whatever came next. She stood at the very brink of the overlook, where the ground dropped sharply into the abyss below. The view was breathtaking, the vast expanse a mirror to her own vast, uncharted future.

Here, at the precipice, Emma paused. The early morning breeze tugged at her clothes, beckoning. She closed her eyes, a single tear trailing down her cheek, lost in the winds of change. Was she stepping forward to embrace the consequences of her actions? Or was she stepping forward into the void, seeking release from the pain that had gripped her for so long?

THE OTHER PASSENGER

Thank you for reading this book. If you have enjoyed it, please visit Amazon, Goodreads or wherever you leave reviews. Reviews help readers to find my books and help me reach new readers.

If you're posting about this book on social media, I'm @jerowneywriter - or @jerowney on TikTok. Tag me!

For further information about me and my work, please visit my website: http://jerowney.com/about-je-rowney

Best wishes,

JE ROWNEY

9 781739 689988